JUBILANT MONTANA CHRISTMAS

BEAR GRASS SPRINGS, BOOK FIVE

RAMONA FLIGHTNER

GRIZZLY DAMSEL PUBLISHING

CHAPTER 1

Montana Territory, Late November 1886

A cold wind howled outside, rattling the shutters. The frigid early winter weather gave little inducement for Leena Johansen, one of Bear Grass Springs' bakers, to rise early from her bed. She snuggled a moment into her husband's warmth before sighing and stretching, readying to travel into town to begin her early morning baking routine. Leena eased away the arm wrapped around her belly as she scooted to the edge of the bed. However, her husband's hold on her tightened, and he tugged her closer to him. "Karl," she whispered in protest.

"Don't go to the bakery. Stay with me." He nuzzled forward and kissed the back of her neck, breathing in the scent of ginger and cardamom.

She turned and held his face between her palms. "You know I have to go to the bakery. I'm already late." She ran a hand through his thick blond hair before kissing him softly on the lips. She gasped as he rolled, pinning her beneath him.

"Stay, Leena, my love," he whispered in Norwegian. He deepened the kiss and threaded his fingers through her long blond hair as he held her closer.

After a few moments she pushed at him, and he fell to his side with a loud sigh. "I don't ask you to cease your work at the sawmill." She paused as he gripped her hand, and she lay beside him, their gazes meeting as their breaths calmed.

"There is little work in winter at the sawmill. I had hoped to have more time with my wife. A belated honeymoon." His gaze became more passion filled as he stared at her in her white nightgown, askew from his recent caresses. They had married in June but had only had a few days away from his work at the sawmill and her duties at the bakery for a proper honeymoon.

"No, Karl," she said in a firm voice. "I love my work at the bakery. Annabelle expects me. Just like you and Karl are business partners at the sawmill, I am Annabelle's."

Any passion in his gaze was replaced by disdain at the mention of Annabelle MacKinnon, the owner of Annabelle's Sweet Shop, Bear Grass Springs' bakery. "You'd choose to spend the day with her over your own husband?"

"It's my job, Karl," she said as she moved to a small curtained-off area to wash before donning her clothes. She brushed her long blond hair and tied it back in a loose bun.

He gave a grunt of disgust but otherwise remained quiet as he lay on the bed. When she moved from behind the curtain to the small dressing area, she frowned to see him still in bed. She shivered as he moved to help her tighten her corset over her full curves, noting his hands failed to rise to caress her shoulders or trace a pattern over her back as they usually did.

She looked at him over her shoulder when he flopped backward onto the bed again, tugging the blankets over him. "I will hope you have a good day."

Her frown deepened as he stared at the ceiling and refused to look at her. She moved to the door, donned her boots, hat, jacket and scarf before firming her shoulders to emerge into the frigid late-November morning.

She lit and hefted a lantern, then stepped outside, where she immediately shivered. A fresh blanket of snow covered the edge of the small porch, and she suspected inches of snow had fallen overnight. Trudging through the fresh snow, she gripped the rope tied between her brother, Nathanial's, nearby home and the house she shared with Karl. A low wind howled, blowing the snow and feeling like tiny ice picks as it hit her skin. She entered her brother's house without knocking, setting down the lantern with a clatter as her body shook.

"Leena," Nathanial said as he rose from the chair in front of the fireplace. "I thought Karl would see you in today." Nathanial Ericson's blue eyes flashed with concern as he beheld his trembling sister. He pulled her into his arms, gifting her with his body heat as she slowly warmed up. "I want you to wait here as I hitch the sleigh."

"Thank you, Nathanial," she whispered. She watched as her brother strode to the door, nearly ducking under the doorway due to his height. Although Karl and Nathanial were tall and slender, Leena stood only a few inches over five feet with a plump figure. She stationed herself in front of the fire, her hands held out to warm them. After a few minutes, she turned to warm up her backside.

When she began to feel warm again, Nathanial poked in his head. "All ready, Leena."

She joined him in the sleigh, bundling under the blankets. "Thank you for driving me in today, Nathanial."

"You know I'm up early every day." He glanced her way, as if she would respond. "Why did Karl refuse to bring you to the bakery again?" This was the third time in a week she had had to ask her brother for help. "Is he ill?"

"He's upset I want to continue to work at the bakery." She kept her gaze downcast. There was little to see as it remained pitch black.

"Then he's a fool, even if he is my best friend. We have little-enough work during the winter, and an income is welcome." He waited as she remained quiet. "There are always periods of adjustment in any marriage, Leena."

"He won't listen to me. He wants me home. Only at home. And he resents everything to do with the bakery."

Nathanial snorted. "He doesn't resent the money you earn." The jingle of the horse's harness sounded in the air, and the horse snuffled, the sound echoing in the still early morning air. "I'll speak to him, *ja?*"

Leena squeezed her brother's arm. "Thank you. Although I know that will only make him angrier." She was silent as she thought about the recent weeks and months of her marriage with Karl. After such joy during their courtship, and a festive wedding, he had become more sullen and possessive as she continued her work at the bakery.

She felt her brother shrug and then was spared saying anything further as they approached town. In the darkness, the shadows of buildings were visible. They passed the school and church on the right while the livery and Cailean MacKinnon's residence were to their left. Soon they came to a halt in front of the bakery, having passed the café, mercantile, Odd Fellows Hall and one of the most popular saloons in town, the Watering Hole. The town was buttoned up, due to the early hour and the frigid temperatures.

Nathanial set the brake and hopped out, tying the horse to a hitching post. He helped Leena down and escorted her to the back entrance where a sleigh could not maneuver.

"Thank you, Nathanial." She kissed his cheek and slipped inside as he nodded and moved away to return home.

Leena smiled an absent hello to Annabelle as she began her early morning preparations for another day of baking. She attempted to put her interaction with her husband from her mind, but their conflict intruded upon the joy she usually found as she measured and mixed her favorite baked goods.

Annabelle MacKinnon appeared as well rested as a mother of a nine-month-old could. Her figure, slightly plumper after the birth of her daughter, Skye, was full, and she had an air of contentment about her. Her black hair was pulled back in a braid, and her light brown eyes were lit with happiness as she moved around her bakery. Although Annabelle had had a rocky start to her marriage with Cailean MacKinnon, they had since found great joy together.

Shortly before they were to open, Fidelia Evans arrived to work. Leena listened to Annabelle tease her sister, Fidelia, and found solace in their improving relationship. Annabelle had arrived in Bear Grass Springs nearly three years ago to find that her sister, instead of on the verge of wedded bliss to Cailean MacKinnon, worked in a brothel. Rather than forsake her, Annabelle continued to try to cultivate a relationship with her. After Annabelle married Cailean MacKinnon, her new family also accepted Fidelia. When Annabelle's brother-in-law Ewan won Fidelia in a poker match a year ago, Fidelia was finally freed of the Boudoir.

Now Annabelle ran an expanded bakery with Leena, as her business partner and fellow baker, with the help of Fidelia, Sorcha and Leticia. Leticia Browne MacKinnon had married Alistair MacKinnon a year and a half ago, and their son, Angus, was born in August. Leticia tended to work the front of the store, selling to customers. Sorcha MacKinnon and Fidelia, besides assisting in the bakery, sold their knitted and embroidered goods to the townsfolk in a special display in the bakery.

Sorcha relished her hours of solitude spinning her yarn and knitting alone at home, whereas Fidelia enjoyed being in the bakery. She helped out by washing dishes, or she embroidered in a corner. Recently she had joined in more conversations the women had throughout the workday in the bakery's kitchen. However, even when Fidelia was silent, her smile or frown showed she always knew what was being discussed.

Sorcha, the youngest MacKinnon sibling and only sister, had been absent from the bakery for nearly a month after suffering a horse-riding accident. Due to the severity of her injuries, she had to recuperate at the Mountain Bluebird Ranch—most often referred to as the MBR. The weather had turned toward winter with a sudden ferocity this year, and Sorcha's brothers had not wanted to risk further injury to her by moving her. Their one regret, now that they knew she improved, was that they could not witness firsthand her interaction with her nemesis, Frederick Tompkins, who owned the MBR along with his brothers.

Leena listened to the sisters' discussion as Fidelia and Annabelle constructed scenarios for Frederick and Sorcha, each subsequent one more ludicrous than the previous. "You know her chattering would drive anyone insane," Fidelia said with a fond smile as she thought about Sorcha. "I can only imagine what that must do to a man like Frederick."

"Who, according to Helen, enjoys his solitude," Annabelle said with a chuckle, her brown eyes sparkling with mischief. Helen Clark had worked on the ranch when she was estranged from Warren Clark before they married. She now lived nearby and worked as the town's midwife.

"Sorcha will be longing for company and won't understand how her constant ramblings will keep away any potential visitors," Fidelia said.

Leena felt her mood lighten at the speculation about Sorcha and Frederick, Leena's initial sour mood now a thing of the past. "I think Mr. Tompkins has more interest in Sorcha than she would like. She'll use her chatter as a defense."

Fidelia smiled. "Perhaps a ranch hand will take a shine to her. That would do Frederick good to know he has competition."

Annabelle giggled. "Have you seen how he's one of the few people who can keep her quiet?"

Fidelia nodded and set a dried bowl on the countertop for Annabelle or Leena to use again. "His comments are just as outrageous as hers, and she's struck dumb by them."

"Cailean would say that's quite a feat," Annabelle said as her smile softened at the mention of her husband, the eldest MacKinnon. They were originally from the Isle of Skye, and he and the next-eldest brother, Alistair, were the first two siblings to immigrate to America. After finally settling in Montana, they had sent money back for Ewan and then for Sorcha to join them. Along with his brother, Alistair, and their partner, John Runs from Bears Renfrew, Cailean owned the livery in town.

As the time neared for the bakery to open, their focus turned from Sorcha to preparing for the daily opening, and Leena tucked away her concerns about her marriage as she focused on baking.

That afternoon Leena trudged home through snowdrifts to the sawmill. She walked in the sleigh track from earlier in the morning, but the wind had wreaked havoc on it, and it was not a clear path. Keeping her head lowered as she passed the livery, she walked as quickly as she could. When she approached the edge of town just past the school, she heard the sound of a sleigh and sighed as she had to step into knee-deep snow to allow the sleigh to pass.

When the sleigh slowed and came to a halt, she raised her gaze to find the MacKinnons' partner, Bears, watching her curiously.

"I'm headed to the sawmill, if you'd like a ride," he said in his deep voice. He was bundled under a heavy coat and hat with jet-black hair cascading down his back. His brown-black eyes were filled with concern.

She bit her lip and then clambered toward him, tripping in her eagerness to be out of the snow.

He leaned over, steadying her and helping her into the sleigh. He nodded to a blanket and then gave a satisfied smile when she tugged it around her. "Seems a long way to walk in such weather," he murmured.

"My husband forgets the time when he is busy at work," she said.

Bears made a discontented sound in his throat. "You should be as important as any work, missus." He made a *click*ing noise and then eased the horse into a smooth trot.

They rode a few minutes in silence before Leena whispered, "Did you really have business at the sawmill?"

Bears gave a huff of breath that emerged as a white cloud in the cold air. "Yes." He paused. "Although my urgency to speak with your brother increased when I saw you looking for your ride as I brought a horse in from the paddock."

She clenched her hands together and nodded. "I don't want your pity."

He laughed. "Good, because you don't have it. You're a resourceful woman, and you have the friendship of many good women. You have no need of any pity." He turned to look at her, his eyes gleaming with sincerity. "It's your husband who merits pity."

She frowned and shook her head. "I don't understand."

"He married a woman he doesn't understand and can't control. He has the most to lose." Bears made a soothing sound to the horse as it stumbled. He cast Leena a quick glance, but she stared at the passing scenery, lost in thought.

The world seemed to have descended into a monochromatic reality of varying shades of white. Everything, from the ground to the tree branches, was covered in at least a thin coating of snow. Oppressive white clouds hung low in the sky, impeding any distant views of the hills or mountains. There was little hope of seeing the sun or a patch of blue sky as the day would soon turn to dusk. The horse's chestnut coat, Leena's blue cape, the green of the sleigh and Bears' buckskin-colored coat broke the monotony of the overwhelming white palette.

"Why were you working in the paddock?" she asked as the silence stretched between them. "It seems too cold for a horse, *ja*?"

Bears grunted and then smiled. "Brutus needed to rid himself of some energy, or he would have busted up a stall. Ewan is tired of repairing them."

"Brutus?" She crinkled her nose at the name.

"Mr. Tompkins's horse. Harold's," Bears clarified, referring to the older man who owned the Sunflower Café with his wife, Irene. They acted like an aunt and uncle to those they took under their wing, especially the MacKinnons. Their grandson, Frederick, ran the ranch where Sorcha MacKinnon was stranded. "Brutus is an ornery beast, and I doubt he'll ever be tamed."

Leena shivered. "It seems no horse is ever tamed enough after what happened to Sorcha."

Bears grumbled his disagreement. "She rode the most docile horse I've ever seen. Something spooked her to throw her as she did."

Leena smiled. "You have trouble blaming the horse."

He looked at her, a smile hidden in his eyes, although he remained straight-faced. "I find that man is more often to blame."

Leena chuckled and rode the remainder of the journey in companionable silence.

When Bears eased the horse and sleigh into the sawmill yard, Leena saw Karl emerge from the building and noted his thunderous glare to find her in the sleigh with Bears. She set aside the blanket, said a hasty thank-you to Bears and jumped down from the sleigh before hurrying inside the small cabin she shared with Karl. She stoked the fire in the stove and removed her sodden socks. She placed them near the stove to dry and donned two fresh pairs in an attempt to warm her feet.

Their cabin consisted of a tiny dining room table which also functioned as a desk that sat near the front door and a window. Behind it was the kitchen with a large stove. On the other side of the doorway was the living area with two chairs, a table and lamp between them. At the rear of the cabin, a curtained-off area held their sleeping area. Their privy was behind the house.

After brewing a pot of tea, she chopped vegetables and prepared a simple stew for dinner. While it cooked in a Dutch oven on the stovetop, she pulled out paper and pen to draft a letter to her mother. Ignoring Karl as he entered the house with a blast of freezing air, she continued to write her family in Norway.

He rumbled around the kitchen, poured himself a cup of tea and then stood over her until she sighed and looked up at him. "Ignoring me never works, Leena," he said in a dark tone.

"But it works fine for you to forget me at the bakery today?"

"It is inconvenient to interrupt my work every day to chase after you."

"Is that what you're doing? Chasing after me?" She took a deep breath. "I work in town. The winter arrived early this year, and it is very cold. I thought my husband would show me the courtesy and respect of coming to drive me home. Especially because you couldn't drive me in this morning."

"This is why you should be home. There would be no inconvenience for anyone."

"For you!" She glared at him. "Why can't you see that working is important to me?"

"And why can't you see that I'm tired of being the laughingstock of this town, *ja*?" His blue eyes flashed with anger. "The man who can't even make enough money to keep his wife."

She frowned and shook her head. "That isn't how it is, Karl." She reached to stroke his hand and forearm, but he jerked away from her. Her eyes flashed with hurt at his rejection of her consoling touch. "Why do you care what others think? The MacKinnon men are not laughing at you."

"They are not men to be emulated! They don't know how to control their women. Look what happened to that sister, running wild because she couldn't control her emotions." He leaned forward. "I will not allow the same to happen to you, Leena. You have until Christmas, and then you are never to work there again."

Her eyes rounded and filled with tears. "No, Karl. We discussed my partnership with Annabelle. You can't mean this now."

"*Ja*," he said with a satisfied nod of his head, as though he had just discovered the perfect solution to their problem. "You have a few more weeks to play with your bakery friends. Then you will be home, where you should always have been."

Leena shook her head. "Why can't you see I can do both? I can work there and care for you too."

"My decision is final. I am your husband." He gave her a severe stare, and she broke eye contact, looking down at her unfinished letter. He moved away to the small living area to read a book.

She sniffled and fought tears as she wrote her mother.

A week later in early December, the scent of cardamom, cinnamon and almond vied for supremacy in the bakery as both Leena and Annabelle baked their special treats. Leena mixed ingredients together in a bowl and watched as Fidelia moved to the front of the expanded display space.

Over the summer, Annabelle had taken on the lease of the empty business beside her bakery, doubling her storefront. With two bakers, Annabelle had thought it made sense to have the space for her and Leena's baked goods as well as to show off Fidelia's needlework and Sorcha's homespun yarns.

"It's wonderful to see her charming the locals in an entirely different way," Annabelle murmured as she watched her sister interact with the townsfolk lined up to purchase their baked goods. Leticia was at home with a colicky Angus. Annabelle shrugged a shoulder in an attempt to free her cheek of flour, smiling when she failed, and focused on her friend Leena. "She's come so far, so fast."

Leena nodded absently as she mixed the ingredients to the point of making her shoulder burn from the rapid movement. She tried to focus on her friend and colleague Fidelia Evans, who had been free of her old life as a prostitute at the Boudoir for over a year and free of laudanum for almost as long.

"What's the matter, Leena?" Annabelle whispered. "I've known for some time that something isn't right."

Leena sniffled and then dropped the wooden spoon into the ceramic bowl with a loud clatter. "I … If I'm to have a harmonious marriage, I am to leave the bakery by Christmas."

"What?" Her friend sputtered and stared as her mouth opened and closed in surprise. "That's … that's preposterous. That's only three weeks from now! We all spoke with Karl about your partnership …"

"Karl is displeased with the amount of time I spend here and has informed me that he expects me at home to perform my wifely duties."

Annabelle blushed and shook her head. "Don't say that too loudly outside the bakery kitchen, Leena. It means other things to most people in town." She raised an eyebrow and fought a giggle as her friend's eyes widened, and then Leena flushed beet red with understanding.

Leena was from Norway, and, although she spoke English well, she sometimes misspoke in ways that had them pealing with laughter. Not today, however.

"What do *you* want to do, Leena?"

Leena shook her head. "As a child, I always thought that I needed to be a good wife first. That anything else was secondary. At least that's what my father taught me." She bowed her head in a guilty manner. When Annabelle remained silent and refrained from any censorious comment, Leena whispered, "But, as I grew older, I changed."

"What would your mother say?"

"I don't know. She was a good wife and mother, *ja*? But she was defiant in her own way." Leena rubbed at her eyebrow. "Taking in washing, working for a wealthy family when we needed money. My father was always persuaded to her way of thinking."

Annabelle sighed and pulled out stools, urging Leena to sit down. "I think you should follow your mother's example. Although that may be hard to do with only three weeks before Karl's ultimatum. However, you need to focus on who you are and what you want. Not on what anyone else thinks you should do and be, Leena."

"I have been married less than six months, and I fear it was the greatest mistake of my life." Her eyes rounded, and she slapped a hand over her mouth as though to trap the words that had already escaped.

"Oh, no," Annabelle whispered. "I had no idea. I thought … I thought you wanted to marry him."

"Nathanial needs him as a business partner. What better way to ensure he remains here than to marry me?" She shrugged. "It is a common practice, *ja*?"

"I thought you cared for him," Annabelle murmured. She gripped her friend's hand as Leena's eyes filled.

"I did. I do." She took a deep breath. "We've known each other since I was a girl, learning to cook and bake from my mother." She swiped at her cheek. "I never thought he would want to marry me."

"Why not?" Annabelle asked with a frown. "You're smart, kind and beautiful. You can cook far better than most. What more could he want?"

Leena shrugged. "He never showed much attention to me until we were here. And then I was excited he was interested in me. I never thought about why he changed. Why he noticed me." She swiped at her nose with a handkerchief. "I know I'm chubby, short and plain. No man's ideal."

"Hogwash," Annabelle said with a growl, reminiscent of the disgusted noises her husband, Cailean, often made, and shared a worried glance with her sister who stood in the doorway. "Do you love him, Leena?"

Leena shook her head as though that were not important. "It's better to be practical than emotional."

Annabelle bit her lip and spoke to her sister. "Did you suspect anything?"

Fidelia nodded. "Yes. I was trained to force a smile and to fabricate joy. I know what it looks like." She stared at Leena. "Are you well?"

Leena frowned at Fidelia's question and then jolted. "Of course. He's not mean. Not like that."

Annabelle sighed, rubbing at her forehead and smearing it with more flour. "But he wants you to give up something you love simply because he resents the time you spend here." She raised an eyebrow, waiting for Leena to respond. When her friend gave a small jerk of her head in agreement, Annabelle shook her head. "What do you want, Leena?" she asked again.

Leena sat on the stool with her shoulders stooped and any of her usual vivaciousness missing. "I want to be brave, like you two. And Sorcha. And Leticia." Her gaze moved between the sisters, including them both in her comment. "I don't know how."

Annabelle was silent a long moment before she spoke. "I won't tell you what to do, Leena. Only you can determine what it is you must do. What I would say is that the patterns established early in a marriage become harder and harder to change as time goes on."

"What does your brother say?" Fidelia asked as she moved to the sink to wash a few dishes during the lull between customers.

"Why should he know anything?" Leena shrugged. "As far as I know, he suspects nothing."

"Your brother is a good man." Annabelle sat staring into space. "He would not like knowing you are unhappy."

Leena emitted a small sound of frustration. "I have no right to be unhappy."

Fidelia wiped her hands on a towel and stood in the midmorning ray of sunshine, warming herself as though a cat while she studied Leena, a woman she considered friend. "Don't you? Why should men have the majority stake in determining our happiness and how we achieve it?"

"I have nowhere to go," Leena whispered.

Annabelle's smile bloomed, and she wrapped an arm around her friend's shoulders. "Now that's where you're wrong. I knew there would come a time when someone would need a refuge. Why do you think I was adamant on having the small back room made larger so that there was a sitting room and a sleeping area?"

"Karl would never forgive you." Yet Leena's eyes shone with hope as she stared at Annabelle.

"You know I don't care. *You* are my friend, not Karl." Annabelle bit her lip. "I fear I'm constantly courting this town's displeasure, and allowing you to remain here will anger many who believe a woman should always remain at her husband's side."

Fidelia's eyes gleamed with humor. "But then you've never courted their favor."

Annabelle smiled. "No, I haven't." She gave Leena a gentle squeeze. "Think about it. You don't have to do anything now."

Leena nodded and returned her focus to the forgotten bowl in front of her, allowing the sisters' conversation to roll over her as she considered her possibilities.

CHAPTER 2

*K*arl sat in their home at the table near the door, waiting for Leena to arrive. He fidgeted in an attempt to find a comfortable position on the too-small chairs. A tall man at over six feet, his large frame caused him to be uncomfortable in most chairs. When the door creaked open, he met his wife's surprised glance with a glower. "Why should you be surprised to see me?"

She set down a small basket from the bakery on the floor for a moment and took off her cape, hat and scarf to hang on a peg by the door. She picked up the basket once more as she moved to the kitchen, where she extracted a loaf of bread and a packet of ginger cookies, and then held her hand over the warm stove, shivering as heat penetrated her cold fingers.

"Answer me, Leena," he said in a low voice.

"Since you didn't pick me up again, I thought you'd still be at the sawmill," she murmured.

"Is it because you wish to avoid me?" He rose and caged her in the area by the sink.

She flushed and bowed her head. "I don't desire to argue with you again. I had a long and busy day at the bakery," she whispered.

"*Ja*, and that is why I wish you to cease working there. I want you

15

home." He frowned as she continued to look at her feet. "Leena? I thought we had agreed to this once we were married."

She shook her head. "You agreed." She took a deep breath and met his confused gaze with a mutinous one. "I never did."

His brows furrowed, and then his jaw clamped with anger. "You tricked me into allowing you to work in the bakery," he growled.

"No, I was never dishonest." She pushed at his arms, forcing him back a step and preventing him from hovering over her. "Stop hemming me in." She met his incredulous stare and raised her chin, instinctively mimicking Sorcha. "We agreed I could work in the bakery to ensure there was enough money to help with winter bills when work was slow in the sawmill."

He flushed red. "That was last year, Leena. Before we married. You are my wife now. I want you home."

She shivered but then shook her head. "No. I want to continue to work at the bakery. I enjoy my work."

"What will happen when a *spebarn* comes?" He flushed, as he rarely slipped into Norwegian, and it was a sign of his agitation.

"There is no baby yet, Karl," she said as she blushed. "And Annabelle has made a room at the bakery to be a nursery. I believe I could continue to work and to care for our baby."

"That damn Annabelle woman," he rasped. "She is a meddler and fills your head with ideas." His eyes narrowed as she blushed a brighter red.

"Don't forbid me from working there, Karl," she pleaded. "I want to introduce the townsfolk to our Christmas food."

"Why should they want to eat *pepperkake* or *julekake*? Why should you care to bake for them?" He shook his head in confusion as he stared at his recalcitrant wife.

She frowned as she met his incredulous, mocking gaze as she thought about selling Norwegian-style gingerbread or the Norwegian Christmas cake to the townsfolk of Bear Grass Springs. "Why can't you understand that I want more from life than washing your clothes, darning your socks and preparing your meals? I enjoy being business partners with Annabelle and working in the bakery. I like my friends!"

"You like them more than me?" he rasped, his jaw ticking with anger. "Have I ever treated you poorly?" He waited until she shook her head. "Have I ever raised my hand to you?" Another headshake. "Do you wish you'd married another?" He waited a bit longer until she gave a faint shake of her head.

He swore and spun away, pacing the short distance to the small sitting area and stood with his back to her. "I don't know what you want from me, Leena." Before she could speak, he turned to face her with an expression of barely controlled rage. "Tomorrow is your last day at the bakery. I am your husband, and that is final. Your loyalty is with me. Not to those women."

"But you said I had until Christmas," she whispered.

"No, tomorrow is your last day. I realize I have been too lenient. Your place is at home." He marched to the door, yanked on his hat and coat, and stormed out the cabin, leaving her alone for an evening for the first time since they had wed.

Leena crossed the distance from her cabin to her brother's house, one hand on the rope to steady herself and to ensure she did not lose her way in the darkness. She poked her head into her brother's home, into what had been her home for a year before she had married Karl. She looked around, remembering the joy and pride she felt as Nathanial had first showed her this finished home. He wanted a well-built residence near the sawmill to show the residents of Bear Grass Springs the importance of purchasing wood from his business. She shivered as she recalled the months they had spent in a temporary sod home when they had initially arrived in Montana from Norway—the constant battle with dirt and dust, and the unremitting fear that the roof would cave in.

Now she moved to the fireplace and stoked the embers. She added kindling and waited a few minutes before tossing large pieces of wood onto the fire. Soon the wood crackled, and the room filled with warmth. She sat in one of the chairs near the fireplace, her gaze distant as she considered her argument with Karl.

"Leena," Nathanial said, his expression remorseful as she started at his voice. "Are you all right? Why are you here and not at home with Karl?"

"I'm fine. I wanted to see how you are."

He frowned. "The same as I was when I drove you to the bakery this morning, *ja*?" He sat in the other chair and contemplated the fire for a few moments. "Why aren't you home with Karl?"

"We fought, and he left." She met her brother's incredulous stare that Karl had left on such a wintry night.

"What is the matter between you and Karl?"

She gripped her hands together and continued to stare at the fire. "He wants me to give up my work. Before we married, he agreed with my partnership with Annabelle. Then last week he told me that I had until after Christmas. Tonight he said that tomorrow was to be my last day."

Nathanial swore in Norwegian. "That's ludicrous."

"Perhaps." She took a deep breath. "Will you still call me sister if I'm defiant?" She raised angry blue eyes to meet his. "If I bring shame on the family?"

He gripped her hand. "You could never bring shame on the family. And, if he is forcing you to take such drastic measures to end your business partnership at the bakery, then I will only ever blame him."

Leena nodded and squeezed his hand.

Nathanial's voice emerged soft and hesitant. "There are things about Karl's past that you don't understand." He met her confused gaze. "Things you don't know."

Her expression turned mournful. "I should, as his wife." She cleared her throat. "It merely proves my point that he married me for convenience. For his partnership with you."

Her brother's grip on her hand tightened, preventing her from rising and returning to her empty home. "No, Leena, that's not true." Nathanial paused and looked away but continued to hold her hand. "But only Karl can explain, *ja*? It's his story to tell."

She raised her free hand and rubbed at the few tears that fell. "It seems I'm not worthy enough for that consideration."

Her brother's harsh words stilled her erratic movements. "Fear can silence a man and make him act like a fool. When the time comes, be kind. Be patient." He released her hand and watched her rise. After a sigh, he rose to match her actions to don winter weather gear to escort her to her cabin. "I refuse to have you lost in this weather."

She nodded her thanks, and they slipped outside for the short journey to the cabin she would share with her husband for at least one more night.

~

The following morning, Leena arrived at the bakery with the basket she had left with the previous day looped over her arm. She groaned with appreciation as she set it beside the back door.

Annabelle raised an eyebrow as she looked at her friend. "Why should an empty basket pose such a burden?" Her inquisitive smile faded as Leena burst into tears. "Leena?" Annabelle rushed to her friend and business partner, pulling Leena into her arms.

After Leena had calmed, Annabelle backed away, keeping her hands on Leena's shoulders. "Why are you bundled up in layers of clothes?"

Leena hiccupped a few attempts at words, but they came out as broken sounds. Finally she spoke. "It was the only way I could leave with more than one outfit."

Annabelle froze, and her grip on Leena's shoulders tightened. "*Leave?* What happened to persuading him through cajoling to your manner of thinking?"

Tears coursed down Leena's face. "He told me last night that today would be my last day. That he was tired of sharing me with the bakery. That my only place was at home, taking care of him." She bit her lip as she bowed her head.

Annabelle pulled her close. "It's all right, Leena."

"I don't know if I'm doing the right thing." Leena shivered and then backed up a step. "The basket is filled with items I didn't want to leave behind."

Annabelle frowned as she studied the benign-looking basket, covered with a checkered cloth. "How didn't he know it was heavier than it should be?"

"Nathanial gave me a ride today. He's not as solicitous as a husband would be, and, even if he suspected, I doubt he would disagree." She shook as another deep, rattling sob burst out. "I don't mean to cause you problems, Annabelle."

"No, come," she said, tugging Leena to the small back rooms. "The bedroom is yours, although during the day I still need a place for Skye, and Leticia will continue to need a place for Angus."

Leena nodded. "Of course. I must remove some clothes before I start to bake today." She headed into the rooms to the side of the kitchen, and she quickly shucked layers of clothes. When she returned to the kitchen, looking at least ten pounds lighter after she had removed three dresses, she donned a crisp white apron. "Can we not speak about this with the townsfolk? I would prefer they not know for as long as possible."

Annabelle nodded. "Of course, although you know that means one or two days at the most. They love their gossip."

Leena bit her lip and then met Annabelle's encouraging gaze. "Could you speak with your sister-in-law and ask her not to mention my departure from my husband's house? A notice in the paper would give me more notoriety than I would like."

Jessamine MacKinnon had married Ewan, the third and youngest MacKinnon brother, the previous December. She was the town reporter. When she had first arrived, she had had a penchant for printing the town's most salacious gossip. After nearly losing Ewan due to such tactics, she had learned that discretion was more important than titillating her readers.

Annabelle gave Leena a reassuring smile. "Don't worry. J.P. isn't interested in this sort of news anymore. I'll see if she wants to write about Norwegian customs or the delicious Norwegian foods you are baking. That will be of far more interest than where you are sleeping."

Leena gave a huff of laughter and rolled her eyes. "I doubt that but thank you, Annabelle." They began to work in companionable silence in the hours before the bakery opened.

Much later the back door opened, and Leticia, the former school-teacher, entered with four-month-old Angus in her arms. From her first marriage, Leticia had an eight year old daughter, Hortence, who was adored by all the MacKinnons and was currently attending school. Leticia smiled at the two women and moved into the back room to place her son in the crib as he slept. She entered the kitchen, frowning as she tidied her hair and dress. "Why are there clothes on the peg and a brush on the table?"

Leena took a deep breath and met Leticia's gaze. "I've left Karl. I'm staying here for a while."

Leticia paled. "Left forever or left for now?" Her blue eyes were huge as she stared at Leena.

"For now, but it may turn into forever." Leena blinked rapidly as she fought tears. "I'm hopeful he will see the wisdom of my wishes."

Leticia patted her friend's arm and then pulled her into a hug, ignoring the flour that would mar her sky-blue wool dress. "If he has any sense, he'll understand what is missing from his life within ten minutes of arriving home tonight to find you gone. He'll do what he must to have you back."

Leena sniffed and nodded.

A few moments later Fidelia burst into the back, a bag slipped over her shoulder. She stilled when she saw Leena near tears and her sister's serious countenance. She set down the bag filled with embroidered items to be sold and clenched her hands in front of her. "So soon?"

Leena met the perceptive woman's glance. "Yes. He told me last night that today was to be my last day at the bakery."

Fidelia frowned. "He won't like it when you don't return home. And he'll dislike the town gossip even more."

Leena shrugged.

"Never discount a man's anger or desperation, Leena. Before agreeing to go back with him, be certain what he says from now on is true, rather than a momentary concession to entice you to return." Fidelia met the women's somber gazes in the room and tilted her chin up, as though expecting them to challenge her.

"Wise advice," Annabelle murmured. She glanced at the clock on the wall near the sitting room door. "We open soon, and there is still much to be done."

The women moved into action, setting aside their concerns for Leena as they baked, prepared trays to tempt the townsfolk and washed dishes. Although they hoped to brighten the day by singing Christmas carols, the dark mood clung to them.

That evening Ewan MacKinnon approached his eldest brother's house, stomping his feet to rid his boots of mud and snow before entering the side door to the kitchen. As the youngest MacKinnon brother, and third of four siblings, Ewan did not work at the livery with Cailean and Alistair and Bears. Instead, Ewan worked as the town carpenter

Before his marriage to Jessamine, he had been a frequent patron and gambler at the most popular saloon in town, the Stumble-Out. Although he no longer visited the poker tables to partake of the games himself, he enjoyed hearing about others' successes as they took risks, either at poker or in life.

Ewan smiled to find his wife, Jessamine, already at the dinner table with a warm cup of coffee between her hands. "'Tis one cruel winter already," he rasped as he shucked a hat, scarf, coat and sweater. He approached the stove and held his hands over the heat pumping from the warm burners.

His wife winked at him as he poured himself a cup of coffee, and he joined her at the table. He smiled at his family gathered around the table and Ewan nodded his thanks as a plateful of food was passed his way. The only absent member was his sister, Sorcha, and he found he missed their frequent verbal sparring matches and her fiery temper. "Any news from Sorcha?"

"Appears she's recoverin' but drivin' Frederick daft," Alistair said with a chuckle. "According to Harold, Frederick wishes he'd never saved her."

"She does have a tongue like a viper when she feels cornered," Annabelle muttered.

"Which I imagine she does daily with a broken leg, stuck at Frederick's ranch," Cailean said. He was unable to hide the concern in his gaze. "I wish we'd been able to get her home before the winter weather struck early."

"You know the doctor advised against moving her," Bears said. "Not if you hoped for her to walk normally again."

The siblings nodded and sobered. "Thank God we have a competent doc in town at last," Ewan said.

Cailean chuckled. "It's humorous to hear the townsfolk complain about him. Seems he's a bit blunt for their liking." He winked at Hortence, who listened to the talk with rapt attention.

"Telling Old Man Fitzgibbons that he's heavy enough to rival a herd of buffalo does little to endear the man," Jessamine said. "That's all the old-timers would talk about today."

Annabelle shook her head. "Our new doctor must learn some tact, or the townsfolk won't listen to him when they really need to."

"Some will always prefer charm and incompetence over the harshness of reality," Bears said. "Remember that, Hortence, and don't be played for a fool when you're older."

Hortence watched him with wide eyes and a fierce concentration, as though attempting to memorize his words. Her red hair never remained in a braid and was often a riotous mess around her face. At eight, she was a bundle of energy and curiosity.

"Well, he was right about Sorcha's injuries," Fidelia said. "Helen agreed when I asked her." The family members all murmured their approval of Helen Clark as she had trained with the previous midwife and had some knowledge about healing outside the birthing room.

"We must be thankful Frederick found her afore the weather turned," Ewan said. "Damn fool. Rushin' out the way she did." He calmed when Jessamine ran a hand down his arm. "Did Harold say anything else?"

"*Nae*, although I think they're concerned about their cattle out on the range," Alistair said. "They're hopin' the weather breaks soon."

Ewan ate another mouthful, before tapping his fork on his plate. He looked around at his family before focusing on Annabelle. "What were ye thinkin', Anna?"

Annabelle shook her head and stared at her youngest brother-in-law in confusion.

"Offerin' refuge to a married woman." He nodded as Leticia flushed, and Jessamine gaped at him.

Cailean raised his eyebrows as he stared at his wife.

"I passed by the sawmill today," Ewan continued, "an' 'twas all Nathanial would talk about. I was lucky Karl didna attempt to skewer me as he does the logs."

Annabelle flushed and then tilted her chin upward. "I was thinking I was aiding a friend who is desperately unhappy."

"She's married, Belle. You have no right," Cailean rasped.

"She is also my business partner."

Cailean rose as their daughter fussed and walked with Skye in his arms but shook his head in disappointment. "Why am I just hearing about this now?"

"I was going to speak with you about it tonight. I had not realized Ewan had already been informed." Annabelle shrugged. "Leena has been upset for a few weeks, but I didn't know why until last week. She was forced to act by her husband."

"'Tis a reckless thing to do!" Cailean said. "Ye've just expanded the bakery. What if the locals decide not to patronize ye any further?" His accent reemerged, as it always did when spurred on by deep emotions.

"Then I will pay for my transgression of being a good and loyal friend," she snapped, lifting her chin higher as her cheeks reddened with her agitation. "There's money saved, Cailean."

"Her husband wanted her to only be at home. To deny her the joy of working in the bakery," Fidelia whispered. She had the tendency to shrink into herself when voices were raised or when there was conflict, yet she spoke up on this matter.

Bears, who had joined them for dinner, said, "To deny her the joy of friendship."

Fidelia nodded. She held her hands clasped together on her lap with her head bowed as she stared at her plate.

Alistair let out a sigh. "She canna remain at the bakery, Anna. 'Tisn't just ye anymore it would affect."

Annabelle glared at the men in her family. "How can you be so weak, so willing to bend rather than standing up for her? She is our friend. She is my business partner, and she is in need. I will not turn my back on her, and she will always be welcome to use the rooms at the bakery for as long as she desires."

Ewan watched her with a calculating glint in his eyes. "That's yer game, is it no'?" When she glared at him, he smiled. "To help Karl see what a fool he is by givin' Leena a place to go."

Jessamine made a small noise of disagreement. "It isn't a game, Ewan. Leena's gambling with her future and her marriage."

He smiled at his wife and nodded. "I ken all about gamblin', love." He raised a worried gaze to look at his family around the table. "I just hope Leena kens it too."

Karl Johansen entered the small home he shared with his wife, Leena, glaring at the chilled stove. His breath formed small puffs of white air in front of him, although it was marginally warmer inside than in the raging winter storm outside. He lifted off the cast iron stove plate, playing with the dormant embers until they came back to life. After adding a few pieces of kindling and then a larger piece of wood, he settled the stove plate atop the stove again. Soon a subtle warmth pervaded the tiny cabin.

He had come home for an impromptu midday meal and had found her letter informing him that she was moving out. He stared into space as his mind replayed her note, his hands fisting with impotent ire.

Karl,

I see no reason to remain when you are unreasonable. I want more from life than to live isolated in this house. I had hoped you would understand that and would celebrate in my success in town as one of its bakers.

For my success is yours, as yours is mine.

Leena

He stared at the stove, glaring at it as it did not allow him to contemplate flames as he would in a fireplace. However, he had been determined to impress Leena and had wanted a proper stove for her since she enjoyed baking. "As though she would be satisfied cooking and cleaning for me," he said with a kick at one of the steel feet of the stove. He listened to the wind howl outside and despaired at his isolation in his small home.

At the knock on his door, he rose and barely spared a glance at his best friend and brother-in-law, Nathanial Ericson. "There is no need to worry," Karl said. "She will be home soon."

"*Ja*, there is. And you're a fool not to realize what you've pushed her to do," Nathanial said as he shucked his coat, scarf and hat. He set a plate of food on the table and met his friend's glare. "You are not eating, Karl."

"I will eat what my wife makes me," he snapped.

"Then you will go hungry and starve like those animals who do not forage enough for winter," Nathanial growled.

Karl turned away and shook his head as he stared at the darkened area of the small living area. At the small bedroom area. "Just say it, *ja?*"

"What did you do to force her away? Why do you believe she left?"

Karl shook his head. "Why do you believe it is my fault? She is not acting like a good woman. A good wife."

"What did you do?"

"I want her home. Tending this home. Tending to our life."

"You know what the bakery and those friendships there mean to Leena," Nathanial said.

"*Ja*, and I know that your family has always been too tolerant of those who should be shunned. Of women who do not know their roles." Karl's jaw ticked as he glared at his friend. "I want my wife at home."

Nathanial met Karl's dark glower. "Are you saying we should never have accepted you, Karl? That my father should never have treated you as he treated me? That my mother should have allowed you to starve?"

Karl spun and stared out the front windows, nothing visible outside in the pitch black.

"This is about you, Karl." Nathanial met his friend's incredulous stare as he spun to peer at him. "*Ja*, you. Keeping Leena here, controlling her, will make you lose all you want."

Karl gave a grunt of disbelief.

"She believes you only married her for the sawmill partnership. That you have no real affection for her."

Karl shook his head, as though Nathanial were a crazy man, spouting nonsense.

"You aren't the only one with doubts." Nathanial took a deep breath. "You risk more than your marriage. You are like a brother to me. But Leena is my sister. She will always come first." He met Karl's irate gaze.

"I cannot be partner with a man who would agree with a woman who abandons her marriage," Karl hissed.

Nathanial's cheeks reddened, and he glared at his best friend. "And I cannot be partner with a man who doesn't know how to cherish what he's been given." He tapped Karl on his shoulder while his jaw ticked with anger. "You'll lament all you have lost." He slammed the door behind him, the windows rattling in their casings worse than from the howling wind.

Karl growled at Nathanial's departing back, tossing the plate of food to the floor in his rage. He stood in the middle of the room with his hands fisted at his side as he attempted to control his anger and welling sense of despair as he faced a night alone.

~

A fire crackled in the potbellied stove as Leena sat in the small sitting room in the back of the bakery. Annabelle had wanted space in the expanded bakery for a nursery and also a place to steal away for a quiet moment from the busyness of the baking. She understood the need for a solitary moment as four strong-willed women worked together on a daily basis.

The small room was painted a soothing yellow and had a rocking chair and another wingback chair around the stove. A desk in a corner was frequently used when Annabelle worked on the books, and a multicolored quilted throw rug crafted by Sorcha hung over the back of the unoccupied chair while a cradle was along a nearby wall. One door opened to the bakery, and another opened to the tiny bedroom. Moonlight shone in through the bedroom's window as the howling wind had dissipated, and an eerie calm settled over the town.

Leena sat in the rocking chair with an afghan over her lap, her hands cupped around a hot mug of tea as she considered her present situation. A letter from her mother sat on the floor beside the rocking chair, and she sighed as she considered her mother's advice.

Do nothing rash, dear Leena. You are in the new moon stage of your wedded life.

Her mother always preferred to speak of nature when giving advice, and Leena wished her mother had chosen to speak more plainly in this instance. Her father, in his few scribbled words, had been blunt.

You knew Karl years before you wed him. Do your duty.

She sighed again, resting her head against the back of the rocking chair and glowered into her teacup. The momentary glow and sense of triumph she had felt at declaring her freedom and her self-worth had faded, and now she sat in dejected silence. Alone and lonely. She rubbed at her upper chest, as though scrubbing away a hidden ache.

Her mind flitted to much-earlier scenes of her life with Karl. Flirting with him as they sat across from each other at her parents' kitchen table in Norway. The anxiety and momentary fear as he waited for her to accept his proposal. Their first kiss, sweet and inno-cent. Watching his eyes gleam with pride and happiness as she had walked down the aisle toward him on their wedding day. The wonder and joy when he had coaxed her from her wedding finery that night. The crinkles at the corners of his eyes when he laughed.

She moved her head to and fro against the back of the rocking chair as tears coursed down her cheeks. Although she had no desire to give up her work or her friendships, she wished she could find a compromise with her husband. "For I do love him," she whispered. "I always have."

A deep sadness enveloped her as she was uncertain her love would ensure her enduring happiness with her husband.

Ewan arrived at the sawmill in a sleigh with his foreman, Ben Metcalf, beside him. With the heavy snow, the roads were impassible for wagons. During the winter months the only possible way to travel was by sleigh. Ewan gave Ben a warning glance. "Don't provoke the man into beating me senseless." He winked at the man he considered partner and then jumped down to enter the warmth of the sawmill. Stacks of cut logs were along one wall, and Ewan scrubbed at his head as he envisioned moving the lumber from the mill to his worksite in a sleigh.

Ben frowned and grumbled, "This is what we get for leaving it until after the snow fell."

Ewan smiled and shook Nathanial's hand. He glanced around but failed to see Nathanial's partner, Karl. "How are things?"

Nathanial shrugged. "Slow as usual in the winter." He looked at Ewan with frank interest. "How is Leena?"

Ewan smiled his understanding, as he had a similar concern about his sister, Sorcha, who he had not seen for a few weeks since the snow fell. "As well as can be expected. I think she hopes her husband will come to his senses."

Nathanial glowered. "That is one thing Karl doesn't have right now." Nathanial ran a hand through his unkempt blond hair.

"Where is he? I thought he'd want to beat me senseless for Anna's actions." Ewan shared a half-amused, half-serious smile with Ben and Nathanial.

"We fought last night as well, and I doubt we'll work together again until this is resolved."

Ben's jaw dropped open. "That's ludicrous. This is his livelihood."

Nathanial's jaw ticked with anger. "Before he stormed out of the sawmill yesterday, I heard him mutter how this morning he might head to Butte to find work there."

"But this is yers," Ewan argued. "Yers and Karl's. There, he'd be nothin' more than hired help."

Nathanial nodded. "*Ja*, but he is very angry that I support Leena over him."

Ewan stared around the sawmill. "Ye canna work this place alone, Nathanial."

"No, and I'm thankful it's winter." Nathanial focused on his friends. "Now, what's the news?"

Ewan shrugged. "Little occurs with all this snow."

Ben laughed. "Now that the MacKinnons are married, and Sorcha is stuck at the ranch, the townsfolk are famished for gossip. They enjoy speculating about Leena and Karl." He raised his eyebrows as Nathanial scowled. "For them, their separation couldn't have occurred at a better time."

"Fools," Ewan muttered.

The conversation turned to the lumber Ewan and Ben needed for the indoor project they were working on, and Nathanial reassured them he could deliver it in a few days.

As they left the sawmill, Ewan sat in quiet contemplation, and Ben whistled a song one of the miners had made popular about a man being punched in the face—"*Two Lovely Black Eyes, Oh, What a Surprise*"—as the sleigh sped along. Ewan shook his head as he imagined all sorts of scenarios for that song title. "Many times in my life …

Aye, that should have been me!" He laughed with his good friend and felt his mood brightening along with the sunny day.

"You should be thankful that wasn't you today," Ben said with a chuckle.

"Aye, well, Leena and Karl must find their own peace. My brothers and I had to. Leena and Karl will too, if he doesna want to lose her." He winked at Ben. "I look forward to the day a fine woman puts ye to the test." He laughed as Ben sputtered, and Ewan continued ribbing Ben all the way back into town.

CHAPTER 3

*L*eena ignored the tapping at the back door for a few minutes, believing it due to the wind rattling the windowpane. However, as it continued, the noise annoyed her, and she wanted to ensure that nothing would break the glass. She peeled away the curtain and gasped as she saw Karl's face on the other side.

"Let me in, Leena," Karl said as he shivered.

"Not here, Karl," Leena said as she tugged her shawl around her.

"Don't make me freeze out here," he cajoled.

"Meet me in the café," she said with a nod of her head to the side to indicate the nearby establishment.

He glared but realized he would not gain entrance into the bakery. After a moment he nodded and departed in the direction of the café.

Leena watched him leave, and she bit her lip before spinning and racing to her small set of rooms.

She changed from her serviceable day dress that she had worn to work in the bakery earlier into the only good dress she had brought with her. She fingered the fine rose-colored wool before slipping it over her head. She brushed a hand over her head to ensure her hair remained in its tidy braid. Glancing in the mirror, she pulled on her coat, hat and scarf for the short walk to the café.

The Sunflower Café was owned by Harold and Irene Tompkins. They were two of the original settlers in the area, and their grandsons owned one of the largest ranches in the valley, the Mountain Bluebird Ranch or MBR. Frederick was at the ranch year-round while his brothers traveled from Texas with herds of cattle in the spring and summer months. This winter, his brothers had opted to winter in Texas. The café had a front room with numerous round tables covered in checkered tablecloths, pictures of far-off places tacked to the walls and a door to the kitchen, where Irene ruled supreme. Harold bustled from the kitchen to the tables, taking orders and chatting with the locals and miners as they waited for their food or nursed a cup of coffee.

When Leena arrived, she saw Karl seated at a back table with few seated around him at nearby tables. She nodded to Harold, who watched her with a curious yet worried gaze as she made her way to her husband. After draping her coat on the back of a vacant chair, she sat.

Before they could speak, Harold arrived with water and cups of coffee. "There's stew or fried chicken. Then you can talk to yer hearts' content. I'll seat any others toward the kitchen on the pretext it's warmer there."

Leena gave a weak smile of thanks. "Chicken," she whispered.

Karl frowned and then nodded to order the same. When Harold left, Karl's frown deepened. "You used to allow me to order for you."

Leena's shoulders slumped slightly. "Karl, why shouldn't I order what I want in a café or restaurant?"

His blue eyes shone with confusion. "Why have you changed?"

She shrugged and fingered a blue thread coming loose from the blue-and-white checkered pattern on the tablecloth. "I haven't. I tried to be someone I thought you wanted." She closed her eyes. "I acted the way I thought you wanted me to act."

He paused for a long moment. "Why?" he whispered. He ignored Harold as he placed two plates of food on the table, focused on his wife, with little interest in food.

"I wanted to marry." She raised her eyes to his. "I've always liked you, Karl. I thought … I thought you would come to appreciate me the way I am. That you'd like having a resourceful wife."

"Is that what you call it?" His eyes now flashed with anger. "I'm the laughingstock of this entire area. I'm the man who couldn't keep his wife happy after six months of marriage, so she moved out."

"Karl," she breathed, "it has nothing to do with that."

"You think my reputation in this town is unimportant? That how I am perceived is frivolous?" He glared at her. "I am seen as less of a man because I can't control you!"

She raised a hand to her mouth, but a giggle escaped. Any levity ended when one of his strong hands slapped the top of the table, causing the plates to rattle. "Anyone who looks at you and doubts your manhood is a fool."

He flushed and shook his head. "You have no idea what you've done to me, Leena."

She picked up her fork and ran it through the mashed potatoes. "Do you even care what you've done to me? All you seem concerned about is yourself, Karl. And that doesn't sound like much of a marriage to me."

His eyes flashed with anger and then hurt. "You knew what I was."

"Yes, as my father wrote me. I knew what you were. An orphaned child, grasping at control so as not to feel so alone and unwanted." She pushed away her plate. "This conversation is going nowhere. Good night," she whispered as she spun on her heel, evading his hand that reached out to grab hers.

Harold stood in front of the exit and herded Leena into the kitchen to an awaiting Irene. "You won't be disturbed in here, and I think you need time with someone who is sensible." He gave her shoulder a squeeze before joining the crowd in the café.

Harold moved to the back of the café, where Karl seemed primed to lunge after his wife. Harold shook his head and pointed for Karl to retake his seat. "You've squandered this opportunity. No use putting into jeopardy the next by acting like an idiot another time tonight and making her want to avoid you for two weeks rather than one."

Harold sighed as he relaxed a bit after a long day of work and faced the young man filled with restless energy. "You bungled that meeting, Karl."

"She was cruel," Karl whispered, his voice laced with shock and hurt.

"When a good woman is backed into a corner, she will strike out. I imagine you pushed her until she didn't know what else to do."

Karl scratched at his head. "I want her home, *ja*? Why doesn't she understand that?"

Harold sighed loudly, this time with exasperation, and leaned forward, resting his elbows on the table. "Oh, she understands plenty well. Why else would she be living in those cramped rooms behind the bakery rather than with you?" He paused as Karl looked at him in confusion. "What you should be asking is why you've acted like a bully and a fool, and what you could do to change."

"I am her husband," Karl snarled. "It's not manly for her to defy me."

"And a fat lot of good that's done you this past week. How are you liking sleeping in a cold bed with little of substance to eat? How do you like having her scent fade from around you, so that it is elusive, and you chase whatever hint of it you can find?" He nodded as he saw a flush limn Karl's cheeks. "Do you think less of me for having a working wife?" Harold asked.

Karl frowned and shook his head.

"Do you look at me and pity me my wife?" Harold tapped his finger on the table. "Early in my marriage, I was fortunate enough to have the good sense to realize what a gift Irene's resourcefulness is."

Harold leaned forward and spoke with intensity. "You are not Leena's master. You are not her owner, Karl. If you had any sense, which I've begun to fear is in short supply, you'd speak with the MacKinnons or our town lawyer. They are strong men, and no one would ever dare doubt their manliness, but they have equally strong wives. Those men are not diminished because their wives have fulfilling lives outside of their homes."

Karl shook his head in confusion. "It is not how it should be done."

Harold closed his eyes and pinched the bridge of his nose. "Think about what I've said. Think about how your wife reacted to your heavy-handedness. I hope, at some point, you'll find a way to some middle ground, or you'll lose your wife forever."

≈

I rene motioned for Leena to sit at the table and placed a smaller plate of food in front of her. "I imagine you ate little with your husband, but you must eat." Irene waited until Leena scooped up small bites of potato before Irene relaxed and sat in the chair across from her. Irene remained quiet until Leena had finished eating.

"Would you like a slice of cake?" When Leena shook her head, Irene poured her a cup of tea and took a sip from her own cup.

After many moments of silence, where the murmur of café patrons filtered in and mingled with the sound of the wind blowing outside, Leena sniffled. "I imagine you are disappointed in me."

"Then you imagine incorrectly," Irene said shortly. "Why would I be disappointed, Leena?"

Leena traced the edge of the teacup and refused to raise her eyes. "I left my home. I left my husband's home." She let out a deep breath. "I know that is not an acceptable manner for a woman to act."

Irene nodded. "Yes, it is shocking to see a woman behave as you have, although I suspect it is mainly because most women wouldn't have a place to seek refuge. Unlike you, they don't have those who would give them a place, and thus time, to determine what they need."

Leena swiped at a tear that tracked down her cheek. "Karl is so angry with me."

Irene nodded again and gave a small *humph* sound.

Leena looked at her friend, her brows furrowed in confusion. "I'm not acting as he expected."

"Just as I suspect he's not behaving as you had hoped." Irene let out a long sigh. "Leena, marriage is a long-term affair. If you are fortunate, the man you marry is a good man and will be with you for years. But that doesn't mean you won't have your trials. Your disagreements." She gripped Leena's hand. "You have every right to show him what you would like, just as he does you."

"I am not acting in a dutiful manner. I should know my place." Another tear trickled out at the words.

Irene tapped her fingers on the table in agitation. "I've never understood why anyone had to have *a place*." She met Leena's shocked gaze. "You are a good-hearted person, Leena. You have never harmed anyone. You have always worked to help those you cared for, perhaps too much." She waited for Leena to meet her gaze and to give a small nod. "Why should another determine what you have the right to do if you are not harming yourself or anyone else and if it makes you happy?"

Leena shook her head.

"Why should he be upset that men, jealous of his good fortune, are besmirching his name, simply because they hope you will choose them the next time you marry?" She watched as Leena's eyes rounded in shock. "Always know your adversary, Leena." She smiled gently. "Don't allow the gossip and spite of others to influence you or your husband."

Leena sat back against her chair, her cheeks flushed. "Why should others imagine I would marry them? I am already a married woman."

Irene shrugged. "In the Montana Territory, it is common for a woman to divorce her husband in the hopes of marrying a man who will better provide for her. Divorce is not hard to come by in the Territory." She saw Leena frown. "Few men would have as much pride as your husband to turn up their nose at a wife who is a talented businesswoman and capable of earning money."

"Pride has always been his problem." Leena scowled into her empty cup.

"Yes, knitted together with a lack of confidence where you are concerned. Your leaving did little to make him feel more secure."

Irene looked up to see Harold in the doorway. She raised an eyebrow in silent inquiry.

"The man's left. As stubborn as my damn horse, Brutus," Harold grumbled as he rubbed absentmindedly at his pantaloon bottoms. His horse, Brutus, had a penchant for nipping Harold in the bottom and ripping away strips of fabric. Even though Bears had worked with the colt, Brutus remained half wild.

"I can't imagine a single lecture by you would change anyone's mind," Irene said with a half smile at her husband's disgruntlement. "Come. Join us."

Harold sat beside Irene and gripped her hand a moment before speaking with Leena. "You have that man of yours tied in knots. And smarting at what you said."

Leena flushed beet red and ducked her head. "I never meant to lash out."

"But he cornered you, and you felt you had no other choice," Harold said. He smiled at Leena's surprise at his understanding. "Your husband is a good man, even if he's a bit of a bully."

"He's had to be to survive," she whispered.

"We all must be at some point. However, now he must learn what he will lose if he doesn't change his ways. I hope he's as smart as I've always taken him to be."

They sat for a few more moments in companionable silence before Leena departed. She smiled her thanks as Harold insisted on escorting her the short distance from the café to the bakery to ensure she arrived safely.

After she entered the small back rooms, stoked the fire and sat in the rocking chair, she stared into space. Her time tonight with Karl at the café replayed over and over in her mind. Unable to determine what she could have or should have done differently, she finally gave up, banked the fire and climbed under the cold covers. As she hugged a pillow to her chest, she fought tears, wishing Karl's arms were around her.

∾

J essamine poked her head into the bakery the following day, sniffing appreciatively as the scents of cinnamon, ginger, cardamom and almond mixed together. "I should write in your spare room just to enjoy the aroma here," she said with a smile.

"Hi, J.P.," Annabelle said as she swiped at her forehead. "What brings you by?"

Jessamine strolled in, her fire-red hair pulled back in a loose bun at her nape. She shrugged out of her jacket and placed her hat over it, although she kept on her scarf. "I was bored."

Fidelia shot her a smile. "No interesting tall tales today?"

Jessamine pulled out a stool on the opposite side of the counter from where the women worked and sat down. "Not today," she said with a groan. "Mr. Kilmarten thought I was naive enough to believe a story about a bear walking on its hind legs." She rolled her eyes at the thought that anyone thought she was dimwitted enough to believe such a tale.

Leena frowned. "I think they can, if only for a few steps. Have you ever seen one?"

Jessamine groaned and dropped her head onto her crossed arms on the countertop. "Why, oh why, did I have to end up here?"

Fidelia laughed. "Because Bear Grass Springs is the exact opposite of those big cities you were running from."

"And you met Ewan," Annabelle said as she bit back a smile.

"I may have to apologize to the old geezer." Jessamine glared at the women she thought of as family, humor rather than anger glinting in her eyes. "I'm checking with Bears to make sure his namesake really can walk two-legged before I have to humble myself to that man."

The room was filled with laughter as they imagined Mr. Kilmarten's delight at Jessamine eating crow. "You'll have to allow him extra time in the storyteller's chair," Annabelle said.

Jessamine groaned. "I'll be forced to take up drinking. He can never use one word when twenty will do." She sighed. "It's why I gave up trying to glean a story from them today and *shoo*ed them away from the fire before they could settle in for another few hours. I decided I could rustle up a story on my own."

"What story could you find here?" Leticia asked as she entered from the front after helping customers. "Except that we are low on Sorcha's wool with little hope of replenishing any of the stock with her out on Frederick's farm."

"Now there's your story," Annabelle said.

"I know, but Ewan forbade me from attempting to ride out there." She frowned and shook her head before she blushed at Leena's intense interest. "Once I got over my anger, I knew he was right."

"How long did that take?" Fidelia asked with a chuckle.

"Oh, a day. He was so worried that I'd borrow a sleigh against his wishes that he asked Cailean, Alistair and Bears to bar me from the livery." She shrugged and then sighed. "I realized I had no desire to be marooned in a ditch, stranded at the ranch or dead from exposure as a storm hit." She glowered as she contemplated giving up researching her story.

"Was it hard for you to admit to Ewan that he was correct?" Leena asked.

Jessamine smiled at the woman who was slowly becoming her friend. "Yes, but apologies are important, and I'd made him worry." She sighed. "I had no desire to be like Sorcha, forcing everyone to join in a search party."

Leticia cringed. "From her letters, Sorcha regrets her rash actions, and she never expected the tamest horse to rear." Leticia shared a look with the women in the bakery. "I think she's more than paid for her foolishness, stuck out on the ranch with Frederick."

"We always knew Sorcha's impetuous nature would hurt her someday," Annabelle said.

"Yes, but I always thought that meant she'd be caught in a compromising position, not actually hurt," Leticia said as she shook her head.

"No, I was the one found in the compromising position," Annabelle said as she laughed, her gaze distant, as though remembering the night of the June dance when she and Cailean had been caught kissing behind the schoolhouse by Mrs. Jameson. "It amazes me that I can laugh about it now."

"You can laugh because it all turned out well," Leena whispered.

Jessamine focused on Leena. "I know the perfect story for my paper. I haven't had a *T&T* in too long. Why don't you allow me to interview you, Leena?" Jessamine had a section in her paper called *True and Tantalizing*, where she wrote about true, unheralded events in the townsfolk's lives.

"There's nothing tantalizing about my life," Leena protested.

"I know what we should do," Jessamine said, sitting straighter as her eyes lit with delight. "Why don't we have an article about what Christmas is like in Norway?"

Leena frowned. "Why would anyone want to read about that?"

Jessamine shrugged. "I'd be as interested in that as I would about Brutus continually eating Harold's pantaloons or a rattlesnake nipping at Tobias last summer." She smiled as Fidelia muttered her dismay at the rattlesnake's poor aim. "You could always talk about what you'll be tantalizing the town with here at the bakery during the Christmas season. Few can get enough of your gingerbread."

"I don't want Karl to be displeased with me for being in the paper," Leena said as she bit her lip.

"Perhaps it will make him nostalgic and desirous of a compromise," Annabelle said while Leticia scurried to the front room as the bell jingled. Annabelle met her friend's worried gaze. "You are honorable and have never done anything to cause him shame. I think a story is a wonderful idea. For you and the bakery," she said with a wink.

Jessamine smiled, snatching a cooling cookie from a rack. "Yes, and I can come by when you're not busy." She closed her eyes in bliss as she savored the bite of gingerbread. "I wish you made these all year-round."

"Then they wouldn't be special," Leena said with a grin.

Jessamine nodded. "And I won't be as big as a house."

The women laughed.

Leena took a deep breath and nodded. "Fine. *Ja.* I will speak with you about Christmas in Norway." She sobered further. "I want nothing scandalous."

Jessamine laughed. "I've no need of scandal when you living at the bakery will keep the town talking for months." She winked at Leena and rose. "I'll be by soon for the interview."

~

Karl poked his head into the livery and stilled as he saw Bears working in one of the stalls. "May I leave my horse here for a few hours?" he asked without preamble.

Bears looked over his shoulder, his astute gaze taking in a bundled-up Karl and showing no shock at seeing him in the livery doorway. He blinked his agreement and returned to work on the horse in the stall.

After a moment Karl returned with his horse, free from the sleigh's harness. He ran a hand over her muzzle and murmured words of encouragement when she snorted, as though in delight to be out of the cold. Her chestnut coat steamed from a mixture of sweat and melting snow.

Bears approached, holding out his hand. He frowned, accepting the reins. Rather than tug the horse into motion, he waited for her to sniff at his hand and to calm down. "Come, beauty," he said in a deep, soothing voice, leading her to a stall toward the center of the barn. "You'll be warm here." He frowned as she limped, and he cast a worried glance at Karl.

"I thought something might have happened on the ride in. She was fine when we left, but then she hitched more to one side about halfway here." Karl hung his arms over the side of the stall as he watched Bears attend his horse.

Bears nodded and ran a hand down the side of her neck as she settled into the stall. "I'll look her over. She might not return with you to the sawmill tonight. But you can borrow one of our horses so you aren't stranded in town." He paused. "Unless you'd prefer to be stranded." He waited to see Karl flush and then stammered a denial. "It would do you good to show as much consideration for your wife as you do your horse."

Karl flushed red and fisted his large hands together.

Bears met his irate gaze implacably.

"I have no need of advice from you."

"Then you are in more need of it than you know," Bears said. "You seem like an intelligent man, lumberman, but I have begun to have my doubts." He waited to see if Karl would storm out of the livery. When he remained by the stall, Bears continued, "Many will be willing to give you advice. I'd be careful to take it only from those who understand what it is to love and to compromise." He shared a long look with Karl. "Or from someone who has loved and lost. For they will advise you so you do not suffer the same."

Karl's gaze filled with confusion as he saw the echo of such suffering in Bears' expression. "I'm tired of being thought a fool."

"Until you value what you have, you are a fool," Bears said.

Karl grumbled and spun on his heels, marching out of the livery into the cold evening air, uncertain of his destination but desperate to escape unsolicited advice.

A few hours later Karl leaned against the battered bar in the Stumble-Out Saloon, sipping a whiskey. The area in front of the long bar was crowded while the gambling tables at the back of the bar slowly filled with those interested in trying their luck. Curtains along the front windows billowed with each howl of wind while the lanterns lit the main area of the room but allowed nooks and crannies to remain dimmed for private conversations or transactions.

Karl watched as men threw down their cards in frustration at Lady Luck's fickleness while other patrons chatted, smoked and spit tobacco on the floor nearby. Karl nursed his drink, unwilling to waste much money at the saloon but equally unwilling to spend another evening alone in his small house.

He stiffened as he listened to the men around him discussing town events. The Second Annual New Year's Eve Dance would soon occur, and many of the men bemoaned the lack of unmarried women. One man muttered that not even Sorcha MacKinnon would be present, due to her injury.

"Makes no sense that the woman had to recover at the ranch. Makes me think something else is goin' on that folks don't want us talkin' 'bout," said one man behind Karl.

"Her brothers are fierce men. They won't allow no hanky-panky to occur," his friend said around a hiccup.

"There ain't no man dumb enough to take on the MacKinnons. Besides, their Injun would scalp you."

Karl snorted and rolled his eyes as he listened to the gossip about the MacKinnons. Karl knew them through Nathanial and his friendship with Ewan. Although the MacKinnons were loyal, Karl could not imagine them doing bodily harm to anyone.

"That foreign baker will be single this year. Betcha we could get a dance outta her." The first man whistled and then slapped his hand on the bar as though that were a compliment to the woman in discussion.

Karl stiffened at the allusion to his wife and forced himself to remain calm.

"Have you tasted the sweet things she bakes?" his friend asked. "I imagine she tastes even sweeter."

Karl saw red and was about to spin to face them when a hand gripped his shoulder, and Karl met Ewan MacKinnon's warning gaze. Although virtually the same height, Karl was stockier. However, Ewan was determined in this moment to prevent a brawl.

"No, Karl. They're no' worth it." He waited until he saw Karl relax before signaling to the barkeep for a drink.

"What are you doing here? I thought you were married."

"The same could be said of you, Norway," Ewan replied with a smile. "Jessie heard of a poker match, an' she wanted the particulars. Sent me to sniff out the tale for her."

"I thought she was the sort of woman who frequented saloons." Karl met Ewan's amused gaze with one of confusion and animosity.

"Aye, she is, an' she's a better reporter than I am. She can recall full sentences, whereas I …" Ewan laughed. "I can remember the basics of a tale but no' the particulars, ye ken?"

"I find that hard to believe," Karl said with a frown.

"So does Jessie. But I believe there can be too much truth in some of her stories. When it comes to a poker match, or an auction at the Boudoir, a little embellishment never hurt anythin'. She doesna always agree." Ewan took a sip of his whiskey and nodded at someone he knew but remained focused on Karl.

"Then why doesn't she come to the saloon for her story? You've admitted she's a better reporter, *ja?*" Karl asked.

Ewan met Karl's gaze and became serious for a moment. "She doesna because I asked her no' to. She understands that I would worry about no' being able to keep her safe should a brawl erupt." His eyes clouded. "We already had that happen once at the Boudoir."

Karl glowered. "Your wife listens to you."

Ewan nodded. "Aye, because I *asked* her and showed her that it was because I cared about her and her well-bein'. No' because I demanded it of her with no rational explanation." He took a sip of his whiskey as he allowed that to sink in.

Karl brooded for a while. When he spoke, he said, "But she still gave up some of her independence to please you."

Ewan laughed. "Do ye think I didna give up as much when I married her?" He shook his head as he looked at Karl. "Jessie kent I was askin' her to give up visits to the saloons, no' because I wanted to control her or to take away an outing she enjoyed. She kent it was out of my concern for her. She decided worryin' me out of spite or in a determination to prove she could do it wasna worth the discord."

Karl frowned. "Your wife sounds more reasonable than mine."

"Ye give, and ye take, Karl. Ye ask for somethin' in an intelligent manner. Ye show her why ye would like somethin' the way ye wish it. If she doesna agree, ye try to see it from her point of view. An' then ye ask again in a way she understands."

Karl shook his head. "I don't understand that type of marriage, carpenter."

Ewan nodded. "I ken. I never kent much about a good marriage.

46

No' until I saw how things were with my brother Cailean an' his wife, Annabelle. An' then, that's what I wanted."

Karl glowered at the mention of Annabelle. "That woman has caused more problems in this town."

Ewan's friendly demeanor changed at the criticism of his sister-in-law. "*Nae*, she hasna. She's helped this town while also showin' more charity to its residents than they deserved. One day, Karl, ye'll be thankin' her for the kindness she showed yer wife." Ewan finished the final sip of his whiskey, slapped Karl on the back and then moseyed over to the area where the poker match was turning serious.

Karl watched Ewan leave, his words echoing through his mind as he finished his drink and then left the saloon. As he stepped outside, he glanced at the bakery. Rather than begin the cold trip home, he crossed the street and ensured the area around the bakery was clear of snow and appeared secure for the night. Whispering into the wind, "Good night, my love," he walked along the boardwalk toward the livery and then rode home.

CHAPTER 4

*A*nnabelle entered the bakery the next morning to find Leena had already baked loaves of bread and was hard at work on her now-famous apple cakes. She made them in small tins so that the miners and townsfolk could buy them as a single-serving cake. This allowed them to sell the apple cakes as a treat, rather than having the customers make an expensive purchase for a larger cake. "You're up early."

Leena stopped stirring her mixture and set her hands on the butcher-block countertop as though she needed the support to remain standing. "Someone was here a little while ago. Outside."

Annabelle nodded. "Yes, they were. And they were quite kind. They shoveled out the back area and left dry wood." She yawned. "Who do you think would do that?"

"Your husband?" Leena asked.

Annabelle laughed. "Oh, he did in the past. When we were estranged, and I was living here. However, I know for a fact he didn't leave our bed this morning." Her contented smile sparked a look of envy in Leena's gaze. "Sounds to me like your husband is attempting to woo you again, Leena."

She huffed out a breath and sat on a stool. "Then he's a fool to believe that shoveling and wood will make a difference."

Annabelle tugged on an apron and pulled out a bowl as she moved to stand beside Leena. "Why? Isn't he showing you, in a subtle manner, that he now approves of your working here?"

Leena shook her head. "I need the words, Anna. I know that may seem small or spiteful, but I need him to say that I can continue to work here." She bit her lip. "My dream is that he says he is proud of what I do."

Her friend gripped her hand. "That is not foolish, to want those we love to esteem what we do. For it is a part of who we are." Annabelle squeezed her hand once more before releasing it. "Give him time. I know he's had numerous conversations with varying MacKinnon men, and I imagine his head is reeling from all of the advice."

Leena half smiled. "Do you think I'm foolish, Anna, for wanting to introduce the townsfolk to my traditions? For wanting to work here?"

"Of course not. I think we are fortunate. And, if the way you sold out of your *pepperkake* yesterday is any indication, the townsfolk are excited to try new things."

"I want to build a *pepperkake* house," Leena said. "It's what we always did at home. And then we can eat it." Her eyes lit with excitement.

"Oh, that's perfect! Warren was just talking with me a few days ago about how they'd like to have a fund-raiser at the New Year's Eve Dance to raise money for the fire wagon. If you baked one of those gingerbread houses, it could be auctioned off. The townsfolk already know how delicious it will be."

Her cheeks were flushed with enthusiasm and her eyes filled with hope. "Do you think they'd bid on it?" Leena asked.

"Yes. We can ask J.P. to print up small pamphlets here for the patrons, so they would know the tradition behind it and how fortunate they would be to make the top bid."

Leena laughed. "*Ja*, I think that would work."

Annabelle gave a little squeal of delight. "Oh, how fun! I'm sure J.P.

will be by at some point today, since she is always looking for a story, and it's been dreadfully dull the past week."

"If she were like she was before she married Ewan, she would write about Sorcha stuck at Frederick's ranch," Leena said. "He always seemed a nice man to me when he was in town in the spring to help his grandparents."

"That's because he was flirting with you to make Sorcha jealous," Annabelle said, earning a shocked stare from her friend. "At least that's what we think he was doing."

"He was never inappropriate," Leena stammered. "Karl would have been very upset had he known."

"It was harmless flirting, Leena, and you didn't even notice it because you were so enamored of your Karl." Annabelle smiled as Leena flushed. After Annabelle finished mixing together the dough for her oatmeal raisin cookies, she paused to look at her friend. Although Leena always attempted to remain positive and upbeat, she now sported dark circles under her eyes, and she lacked her usual vitality. "Why don't you speak with him?"

Leena frowned in confusion. "Why should I speak with Frederick? He's at the ranch." After a moment her gaze cleared, and she looked away. "What should Karl and I speak about?"

"What matters," Annabelle murmured. "You've shown him what you want. You've shown him that you can live apart. But do you want your separation to continue? Do you want to live away from him forever?" When Leena remained silent, Annabelle shrugged. "For, if you do, you should speak to Warren about obtaining a divorce."

Leena reacted as though she'd been sucker punched. "No, never that."

"Then you must do something. You can't continue to hide here, refusing to leave, barely going to the café for fear you might see him." Annabelle scrubbed at her forehead, swiping it with flour as she always did when she baked. "Be brave, Leena. Face Karl and your fears. For you already know what the worst could be."

Leena raised wounded, devastated eyes to meet Annabelle's gaze. "Yes, a life without him."

Annabelle fought her own tears as she clasped her friend's hand. "Yes."

~

The following evening, Leena looked at the scene she had prepared in the bakery. She had transformed the butcher-block countertop into a makeshift table. A fine cloth covered part of it, with the table set for two and candles lit. The scent of roasting chicken, rather than baking bread, filled the kitchen. Karl and she would sit looking across the counter from each other, with her goal to talk with each other.

She fought wringing her hands together but failed as the hour of his arrival came and passed. She straightened an already straight fork beside one of the plates and then sat dejectedly on a stool as the candle wax seeped down the side of the candle and onto the tablecloth. She sniffled and then rose to take the chicken from the oven before it burned to a crisp.

At the loud knock on the back door, she set down the chicken and then moved to the door. Unable to ascertain who stood outside, she eased it open. "Karl?"

"Are you expecting someone else?"

"No," she whispered, suddenly shy. She stepped back, and he entered, covered in snow, ice clinging to his eyebrows and hair. "Oh, you're freezing," she whispered as she raised her hands to cup his reddened ears. She blushed at her impulsive action and moved to drop her hands, only keeping them in place when he held them there.

"That feels like heaven," he whispered as his eyes closed.

After a moment she tugged away her hands. "Get out of your wet clothes, and stand by the large oven. Warm yourself over there."

He looked at the romantic scene and froze. "Leena?" He shook his head, sprinkling icy water on the floor. "I thought we would go to the café for dinner."

"I want us to talk without interruption or as others gossip around us. Harold and Irene are nice, and I've enjoyed their support." She met his guarded gaze. "But I don't want them to interfere tonight." She gripped her hands at her waist as he remained quiet, staring at her. "I hope that is all right." She relaxed as he smiled broadly at her.

After hanging his coat, hat and scarf on a peg by the door, he headed to the stove. "Heaven again," he whispered as he closed his eyes while the warmth permeated him. He shivered violently a few times as though his body fought giving up the cold it held within, and then he relaxed. "Ah, I already dread going back out in that storm."

"Come. Enjoy dinner before it cools too much," Leena urged her husband. She motioned for him to sit on the side near the oven to continue to warm up. After serving their simple meal of roasted chicken, potatoes and root vegetables, they ate in silence.

"Why did you want to see me, Leena? We aren't talking, if that was why you wanted me here."

She set down her fork with a clatter and darted a glance at him. "I wanted to see if you still feel the same way." She frowned at her whispered words.

He took another bite of his meal before pushing away his fork and plate. "I will not lie to you, Leena. I do. I want you home."

She frowned. "You want me home to be only with you, or you want me to return home to live the life we were creating?"

He sighed and clenched his hands together into tight fists. "I don't know," he whispered. "I wish I did."

She smiled, and he watched her in confusion. "Thank you for not lying. For not promising me that you've changed just to have me return, when you are still uncertain."

He nodded. "If I've learned one thing, my love, it is that I hate living alone. I miss you singing in the kitchen. Your scent. Your small touches as you pass by me." His eyes lit. "I miss holding you in my arms at night."

She nodded. And, rather than appear encouraged, she looked miserable. "I know. I miss your deep voice. Your laugh. Your stories." She sniffled. "I don't like this disagreement, Karl."

"Then come home," he urged, reaching forward to grip her hand.

"I can't. Not until I know we are in agreement about my work."

She tensed as she expected him to rise and pace and rail at her. Instead, he sat in quiet contemplation before nodding.

"*Ja*, you're correct." He rose with reluctance. "I don't look forward to the return trip to the sawmill tonight." With that, a loud gust of air rattled the back door and windows.

Leena rose and opened the door to peer outside. She shrieked as a pile of snow cascaded inside, and she jumped backward. An icy gust burst into the room, and she pushed with all her might to slam the door shut around the snow and wind, to no avail.

Karl stood behind her and, with minimal effort, slammed the door shut. He chuckled and then stilled as he inadvertently had Leena in his arms for the first time in over a week. "Are you well, my Leena?"

"Karl," she whispered, turning into his arms. "I ..." She raised a hand to trace his whiskered cheek. "You can't travel home in this tonight."

He nodded. "I can sleep at the livery or rent a room at the hotel."

She stared into his eyes and shook her head. "No, you'll stay with me tonight." She shook her head to dampen the hope rising in his. "I can sleep in the comfortable rocking chair."

"No," he growled. "Let me hold you again, my love." He bent forward, brushing his lips against her hairline and then down the side of her cheek. "Let me dream."

"Nothing has changed," she whispered.

"But it has," he countered as he pulled her into his arms. "We are talking rather than fighting. There is hope again."

She let out a shuddering sigh and gradually relaxed in his powerful arms. "*Ja*, we have hope again." She rubbed her cheek against his chest and clasped her arms more tightly around him. "I've missed this. I've missed you."

"Are you sure?" he whispered, doubt present in his voice.

She pushed back to trace her fingers through his hair and then down his face. "*Ja*."

His eyes were tormented as he stared deeply into hers. "You doubted marrying me." His expression became even more serious as she flushed and broke eye contact. "Leena?"

"The man you were becoming wasn't the man I thought I'd married," she whispered. "You were a brute, trying to break my will." She blinked as she fought tears. "I take pride in what you do at the sawmill. Why can't you be proud of what I accomplish here?"

He stared at her dumbstruck a moment before his hold on her tightened. "I am proud, Leena. It's my pride that is the problem."

She shook her head and then shivered as the melting snow seeped into her slippered feet. "Come. Let me clean up the snow, and then let us retire."

He stilled her erratic movement away from him. "Together?"

She met his hopeful expression. "Yes, together."

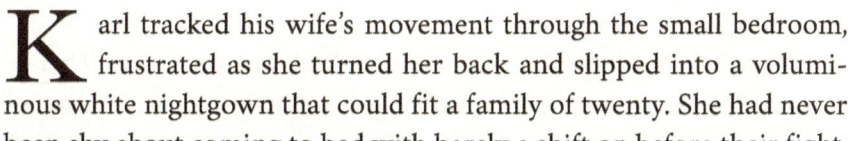

Karl tracked his wife's movement through the small bedroom, frustrated as she turned her back and slipped into a voluminous white nightgown that could fit a family of twenty. She had never been shy about coming to bed with barely a shift on before their fight, and he found something else to mourn in their marriage.

"Why are you frowning?" she whispered as she brushed her hair before deftly braiding it and tying it with a ribbon.

"That ugly nightgown," he said with a roll of his eyes in disgust before he flopped back onto the bed.

Leena giggled. "It's a hand-me-down from Irene. I didn't leave with much."

Karl rolled to his side and propped himself up on one elbow. He had shucked his clothes, leaving them near the potbellied stove to warm overnight and only had on his underclothes. His strong arms and chest muscles caught her attention as he moved, and he smiled. "Come, Leena." He held out his hand to her, frowning as she bit her lip and hesitated.

"I think it would be better if I slept in the chair."

"Love, sleep in my arms tonight," he coaxed.

She flushed and looked down, her braid flopping over one shoulder and reaching to her breast. She remained standing near the bed but too far from him to touch her while laying or sitting on the bed.

He threw back the covers, shivering as the cool air hit his skin, even though the air had been warmed by the stove. "Leena, what have I done?" He eased out of the bed to stand before her and traced a finger along her neck to her shoulder, stilling his movement when a tear tracked down her cheek. "Do you want me to go?"

She lowered her head. "You'll think me ..."

"What, my love?" he whispered as he bent over, breathing in her scent of ginger and cardamom as he kissed her head.

"Shameless."

He froze at her breathed word. "Leena?"

"I want to make love with my husband," she said as she lifted her head and met his shocked gaze. "Even though we aren't reconciled, and I'm not moving home."

He smiled and cupped her cheeks, chasing away her tears. "There's no need to cry, my darling, for wanting me. For loving me," he whispered, the last said with hope in his voice.

"I should want to wait until we are fully reconciled," she said, swaying toward him and his soothing touch. "I should be able to restrain this want. I should ..."

"Enough with the damn *shoulds*," he rasped, swooping down and kissing her, the kiss demanding and passionate. He groaned as she stepped forward, pressing against his front and wrapping her arms around his neck. He shivered as her fingers traced over his muscles, and he pulled her even closer.

After a moment he spun her, laughing with her as they toppled onto the bed.

She pushed at him until she draped over him, and she pulled back farther, her fingers seeming to map each of his muscles. He arched up for more of her gossamer-soft touch when she sat up fully, easing herself off him.

"No, my Leena, don't go," he gasped.

He stilled his frantic grasping for her and silenced his begging when she looked at him with a passionate intensity and a mischievous look in her eye. She scooted up on her knees, hitching the large night-gown over her hips. She shivered as his hands caressed her thighs, and then she lifted the gown upward and over her head, tossing it to one side of the bed. She groaned when his hands rose, brushing over her breasts.

"I've missed you so much."

As he rose up, kissing her neck and collarbone, she threw her head back, before he rolled her so she lay with him over her.

Her fingers brushed away a lock of hair that hung over his fore-head, and she leaned up, kissing him softly. "Love me, Karl. Love me like you used to," she pleaded. She smiled as he groaned.

"With pleasure, *min kjærlighet,*" he whispered as he kissed her neck. He fell into further passion as he slipped into Norwegian for "my love." Rather than continue to speak in English, he returned to his native language to whisper to her, between kisses, how beautiful she was, how much her passion pleased him and how much he had missed her.

~

Leena stirred when she felt Karl slipping from the bed. "No. Don't leave me yet." Her hands reached out from under the covers, tracing along soft skin as he moved from her. She peeked over the pillows in confusion as he chuckled.

"I'm putting out the candles, darling. I don't want to start a fire." He blew them out and then banked the fire in the little stove before crawling into bed again with her. He hauled her up against him, shivering as she warmed him after his short walk around the tiny bedroom. "I'd hold you forever if you'd let me."

"Karl," she whispered, "why is it so important that I remain at the house?" She rubbed her cheek against his chest as his fingers played with her hair, now loosened from its braid.

"You know what my childhood was like, Leena," he said in a soft voice as they listened to the wood crackling and the wind howling outside.

She pushed up and attempted to see his face in the deep shadows of the room. "You were an orphan, taken in by the Johansens. You spent as much time with Nathanial as you could. I can scarcely remember a day you weren't at a meal with us."

He nodded. "Did you never wonder why?" He held her face between his palms.

"I always thought it was because they were old, and you liked our company better."

"I did my chores. I kept their farm running. But I was never their son. Never their family." He shook his head. "Not after I refused to allow them to turn me into Bjorn." He spat the name as though it were cursed.

"Bjorn?" Leena whispered. "Their dead son?" She frowned when he nodded. She had never known Bjorn but had heard a lot about him from her family as their farm neighbored the Johansen farm in Norway. "But you're nothing like Bjorn."

"I know," he said in a harsh whisper.

"No, what I mean is that he was fragile and bookish and quiet. Everyone talked about how he never would have been able to do the farm work and how fortunate the Johansens were to adopt you." She shook her head in confusion. "You're brawny and strong and filled with life."

His blue eyes gleamed with years' worth of pent-up anger and impotent rage. "When I was chosen to leave the orphanage, I was happy. Few children older than one or two are chosen until we're old enough to work a farm." He paused. "But I was chosen when I was eight."

She frowned and bit her lip. When he looked at her in confusion, she whispered, "How many other boys were eight at the orphanage?"

"None."

She cupped his face. "Bjorn was eight when he died. Did you meet the Johansens before you arrived at their farm?"

"No, I was sent there after a letter arrived at the orphanage."

Her gaze grew mournful. "What happened after you arrived?" She ran her fingers over his shoulders as though reassuring herself that he was well. "Karl? What did they do to you?"

"Mrs. Johansen slapped me. Said I was nothing like Bjorn, and I had to learn my place." His gaze was distant. "I didn't know what she meant. I thought they had wanted *me.*"

Leena's eyes filled at those revealing words. "What did you do?"

He shrugged. "At first, they wanted me to act like him, speak like him, dress like him. When I didn't, I earned a whack with the cane. Soon I was big enough that I broke the cane in half." He paused as he let out a deep breath. "Then Mr. Johansen ceased speaking with me. I was no more than a laborer to him. She"—his voice filled with loathing—"*she* decided I should not eat. I was not Bjorn and refused to replace him for them. Her Bjorn was dead and not eating, and thus I shouldn't either."

Leena raised a palm and traced it over his brow. "Which is why you always were at our house for meals. Why you always had a neighboring fence or animal to work on at mealtime."

"*Ja.* Your mother suspected and never complained about making her food stretch for another. Even for another as hungry as I was. Growing boys eat so much."

"Oh, Karl," she whispered, wrapping her arms around him and laying her head on his chest again. "I hate that you were shown such little kindness."

He kissed her head. "But I was," he whispered. "By your mother. Your father. All of you. You never looked at me and wished I were different." He pushed her back until they were looking at each other in the shadows. "Until I asked you to stop baking." He shivered.

"What?" she whispered.

"You looked at me like she did," Karl rasped. "Like Mrs. Johansen."

"How did I look at you?" She furrowed her brows as she stilled her hands. She wanted to focus on this conversation, rather than provoke any ill-timed passion.

"As though I were wanting. As though I could never be what you truly desired."

She saw a fleeting flash of hurt and devastation in his eyes before he closed them. She sat there, perched on his chest as her mind raced at what she had unwittingly done. "Karl, you tried to take away something that brings me great joy. For no reason I could understand. I was angry."

"When I asked you if you were upset to have married me, you paused before saying no," he said. "You paused, Leena."

"In that moment I was upset, and you weren't acting like the man I thought I knew." She traced her hands over his chest.

"Are you upset to have married me?" He shifted in an attempt to better see her. When the silence lengthened, he pulled her so she lay on her side and off of him.

"Karl," she whispered, "when we are like we've been tonight, of course not. But we've resolved nothing."

He rose, pulling on his clothes, his movements jerky. "I've listened to the advice. I'm trying to understand your perspective." He crawled around on the floor as he searched for his socks. "I resent that you won't do the same for me."

"Karl," she stuttered out as her throat clogged with tears. "Please don't go. Not when there is so much more to say."

He spun to face her, his shirt misbuttoned, his hair on end and his eyes blazing with anger. "You paused again, Leena." He shook his head. "Know your answer when I ask you the third time. For there won't be a fourth."

He tugged on his half-dried boots, marched out of the room and, after a few moments where she heard more rustling of clothes as he pulled on his jacket, the rear door slammed shut. She rose, tiptoeing across the freezing floor to flip the lock on the back door before racing to her bed. She pulled the covers around her, tugging his pillow to her to breathe in his scent.

"Fool," she whispered as she cried herself to sleep.

CHAPTER 5

*K*arl eased open the barn door, hoping not to cause any sound. The interior was darkened, and he stumbled down the inner aisle of the barn. Although cold, it was much warmer than outside with the heat the animals supplied. Rather than attempt to find a lantern to light, Karl found an empty stall with fresh hay and bedded down for the night, tugging his coat around him.

He jerked awake a few hours later when his leg was kicked, and he jumped to his feet, fists ready for a battle. He relaxed when he saw Bears watching him curiously. Karl scratched at his head, pulling pieces of hay from his blond hair.

"I never expected to find you here, lumberman," Bears said. "Thought you had more sense and would spend the night with your wife."

Karl nearly growled at Bears, earning a grunt of understanding.

"At least you tried," Bears murmured before he moved away to the tack room. "There's breakfast in the main house, if you're hungry. They always have food for ten."

Karl rubbed at his grumbling stomach, remembering he hadn't eaten much of last night's supper due to his attempted reconciliation with his wife. He looked for Bears to thank him, but he had disappeared into the tack room. After Karl grabbed his hat, he walked the short distance from the livery to the main house. Rather than barge into their kitchen, he knocked on the door.

Fidelia Evans opened the door with a confused smile. "How may I help you, Mr. Johansen?" Her chestnut-brown hair was tied back in a bun, and she wore an apron over a sky-blue wool dress that matched her eyes.

He pulled off his hat and rubbed at his hair, flushing as more pieces of hay flitted out. "I ... Bears told me that I might find some breakfast."

"Did you sleep in the barn?"

"*Ja*," he said, his jaw firming as though expecting criticism.

"Next time, knock on the door. You could have slept in the parlor. And Sorcha's room is unused right now." Fidelia opened the door fully and allowed him inside. The large stove heated the kitchen, and a blanket was tacked over the door leading to the front hallway to keep the warmth within the room. In the half of the room that served as the kitchen, there was a large stove, a sink with a hand pump, an icebox and cabinets for holding plates, serving dishes and china. A round table with six chairs sat in the other half of the room with a cheerful red-and-white tablecloth covering it.

He shook his head in consternation. "I don't understand you." At her raised eyebrow, he let out a deep breath. "You give my wife a place to live away from me, but you would also give me shelter?"

Fidelia frowned as though disappointed in him. "It was the middle of a blizzard, Mr. Johansen. There are few we would turn away." She motioned for him to sit and then poured him a cup of coffee. Soon a plate of eggs, ham and potatoes with a piece of buttered toast was set before him.

"Thank you," he said as he waited for her to sit. "I only have breakfast like this on the days Leena doesn't work."

Fidelia gave a sniff of disgust. "That's no reason to keep her tied to your house. Your wife has a skill that she enjoys sharing with the townsfolk, Mr. Johansen. I hope you will take pride in what she accomplishes."

He paused and stared at a woman he knew he should scorn but who sat with great propriety with him at the table. "What has she accomplished?"

"She ran the bakery when Anna had her child. She runs it alone on days Skye is ill or when Anna is too tired to bake. Leena has introduced the town to her favorite Norwegian baked goods and has them clamoring for more." Fidelia smiled. "This is a group of people who think that pepper is an exotic spice, and now they are excited about gingerbread and the use of cardamom in their breads."

Karl frowned and listened as Fidelia continued to speak. He ate but barely tasted the food, his focus on the information he learned about his wife.

"She knows every customer by name, even though she is rarely out front. She only has to meet someone once, and she will remember them. Then she charms them, and they buy more than they had planned. And they return the next day to the bakery, delighted with what they had purchased." Fidelia paused as she half smiled. "The best thing Anna ever did was hire Leena as a partner. She is a hard worker, funny and intelligent." She looked at Karl, sobering. "And loyal."

He paused in eating. "What do you mean, Miss Evans?"

Fidelia leaned forward, her cup of coffee ignored. "Do you believe that your wife hasn't had more than one indecent proposition in the time she's worked at the bakery? Many men would be eager to marry such an enterprising woman."

Karl shook his head. "No. When I go to the saloon, they tell me that I am the man who can't control his wife. That I am a joke of a man."

Fidelia looked him up and down, and shook her head. "I know men, Mr. Johansen, and you are no laughingstock." She paused as she flushed. "Are any of those men your friends, or do they sidle up to you with a glass of whiskey and act like they are delighted to make your acquaintance?" At his nod, she glowered. "Have you no experience in this world?"

He sputtered, but her glare silenced him.

"Those men are cunning. They want discord in your marriage.

They hope you and Leena will divorce. And, if not divorce, that she will be so miserable that she will look for consolation outside of her marriage."

"Why would anyone do that?" he asked as he shook his head in confusion.

"Men will always covet what another has." She shrugged. "Well, most men. I've met a few who aren't that bad." She waved away that concession and said, "Who wouldn't want a woman who can cook better than most? Plus they see how successful she is and can imagine how much she earns. What man wouldn't want that? Especially a miner who is working hard to earn nothing?"

Karl sat back in his chair as though he had been poleaxed.

She pointed at him, her expression one of defiant earnestness. "You should have your own good reasons for Leena not working in the bakery. But have them be valid. Have them be *your* reasons. Not some trumped-up excuse fed to you by drunken miners envious of your wife and what you have." She rose, waving at him to remain seated. "I must go to the bakery. I hope you have a good day."

He watched her depart, his mind whirling by what she had said. After another swallow of coffee, he rose to return to the barn to hitch his sleigh.

Ewan poked his head into the livery, surprised to find Karl Johansen striding up and down the central aisle as he waited for Bears to curry his horse. "It's included in the cost, and ye might as well save yer energy," Ewan said as he leaned against one of the posts. He caught Bears' gaze and fought a smile.

"I need to return to the sawmill," Karl snapped as he continued his pacing.

"What ye need to do is speak with yer wife, no' tramp around like a fool," Ewan said.

Karl spun to face him, his arm striking out as though to pummel Ewan.

Ewan dodged the blow and held up his hands in a placating manner.

"Don't tell me what to do with my wife. I'm tired of all the advice, *ja*?"

Ewan nodded and kept his gaze on the irate man, although he noted that his brothers now stood behind Karl, poised to aid Ewan were it necessary. "I never meant ye any harm, Karl. When I acted like a daft idiot about Jessamine, I needed advice too. Ye may no' like what ye hear, but that often means it's what ye most need to hear."

Karl dropped his hands and spun over to the stall where Bears had finished readying his horse. Karl jerked on the bridle, earning a growl of displeasure from Bears, and led his horse from the stall and out of the livery to hitch it to the waiting sleigh.

"Damn fool," Cailean muttered as he marched to the livery door and shut it after him.

"He's actin' no differently than we did," Alistair said. "His wife has him tied in knots, and he doesna ken how to untie them."

"He'll have to learn, or he'll ruin what he has," Bears said as he moved to the tack room.

Cailean turned and focused on his youngest brother. "What brings you by, Ewan?" At thirty-eight, Cailean acted as the family patriarch, although he often needed his brothers' counsel.

"I'm worried about Jessamine," he murmured as he sat on one of the stools near the closed door that led to the paddock. He paused and nodded his thanks as his brothers remained quiet as he thought through his concerns. "I think she might be expectin' our bairn."

Alistair slapped him on the back. "Wonderful."

Cailean frowned. "Why aren't you celebrating? Shouting it to all who will listen?" He watched his youngest brother fidget, and his concern intensified. Quiet worry was not how Ewan usually responded to joyful news.

"Should I wait for her to tell me or talk with her about what I suspect?" He rubbed at his face. "I'm no' sure she wants a child. No' after the way her father treated her."

Alistair reared back. "But that wouldna be fair to ye or to her. Why deny yerself the joy of havin' a child merely because ..." His voice broke off as he looked at his eldest brother.

"Because of fear," Cailean murmured. "One of the best days of my life was when Belle told me that she was expecting our child. Our Skye. I think it meant a lot to her to be able to tell me, in her own time. I think you should trust in J.P. Give her the time she needs now and then celebrate your good fortune."

Ewan nodded. When he met their gazes, his was filled with cautious hope. "I want to be a da so much."

Cailean squeezed his shoulder. "Aye, I ken," he rasped as a deep emotion overcame him, allowing his suppressed Scottish accent to emerge. "Ye're a wonderful uncle, and ye'll be a fantastic father."

Alistair smiled. "If what ye suspect is true, ye'll have much to celebrate this Christmas."

Ewan smiled and then rose, clapping each of his brothers on the back. "Dinna tell yer wives." He saw them frown and then nod in agreement. After a few more moments Ewan slipped from the livery to return to the house he worked on.

True and Tantalizing

Have you become as addicted to Leena Johansen's gingerbread as I am? Do you dream of apple cakes when you wake? Does the prospect of learning she has more Norwegian Christmas delights to share with you fill you with joy? If so, then this is for you.

Leena arrived in Bear Grass Springs in 1883 with her brother, Nathanial Ericson, and family friend, Karl Johansen. They lived in a sod house their first year here as they built their new house and Karl's separate cabin and reestablished the town's sawmill, previously destroyed and abandoned in a fire. During her solitary time, Leena pined for her family in Norway. For the times she cooked with her mother and four sisters. For the camaraderie shared among women.

Thus she began to bake Norwegian delights. She badgered Mr. Sutton until he ordered the spices she needed. When she inhaled the scent of cardamom for the first time since leaving Norway, a small ache in her heart healed.

Now, as Christmas approaches, she will prepare her favorite dishes, for you and for the gnomes that keep her home safe from mischief. The Nisse also bring small presents on Christmas, so she likes to keep them happy.
Leena will make her gingerbread, known as pepperkake, *and will remember her mother teaching her how to mix the batter when she was a girl. She will prepare the traditional hot rice pudding, or* risengrynsgrøt, *and leave a bowl out for the friendly gnome living in the barn and protecting her animals. If you are fortunate, she will share some with you, so your home will be equally protected. Her special Christmas cake, the* julekake—*filled with candied peel, raisins and the exotic spice cardamom—will be baked with the echoes of the times she shared just such a cake with her family, sitting around her family table in Norway. Her baking will enrich your holiday season, as Leena's presence has enriched our town.*

At home she will have a special candle lit for each night between Christmas and New Year's. Her Christmas tree will be decorated with julekurver, *small paper baskets in the shape of a heart. And she will wish all she meets,* God Jul. *Merry Christmas.*

~

Leena looked up expectantly from kneading dough when Fidelia entered, Leena's shoulders stooping with regret at her friend's arrival.

Fidelia looked at her and then nodded as though understanding her sadness. "He's not coming, Leena. He ate breakfast, and I think he's returning to the sawmill." She frowned as Leena's eyes filled.

Leena backed away from the bread she kneaded and grabbed a handkerchief from her pocket to wipe at her face and nose before washing her hands. She placed the bread in greased bowls and covered them with clean cloths for the first rise. "I'm such a fool."

"Why?" Fidelia asked as she pulled on an apron and moved to the sink to wash the early morning bowls and pans.

"I thought the worst thing was to be barred from working at the bakery," she said around her tears. Even though she swiped at her cheeks, the tears continued to fall. "I was wrong."

Fidelia sat on a stool beside her friend, the dishes in the sink forgotten. "What is worse?" When Leena stared at her like she was related to the village idiot for not intrinsically understanding, Fidelia said in a low voice, "I've worked so hard for what I have now. My self-esteem. My needlework that I sell. I can't imagine being denied that."

Leena sighed and sat facing her friend. "What if you were offered love and threw that love away not once, but twice?"

Fidelia smiled and shook her head. "I know you didn't do that, Leena."

She looked at her friend with wide guilt-ridden eyes. "But I did. I hesitated, both times, when he asked me if I regretted marrying him." She frowned. "When he asked if I was upset I had married him."

Fidelia played with a stray piece of drying bread dough. "Why did you hesitate?"

Leena dropped her head onto her arms. "When he's the Karl I remember from when I was a girl or when we first married, I'm happy I married him. But there are times he's resentful and angry and jealous. I don't like him then."

By this point Fidelia had formed the discarded bread dough into a small ball in her hand, and she rolled it around. "Why does he act that way?" At Leena's blank stare, Fidelia asked, "*When* does he act that way?"

"I don't know."

"Of course you do. You need to pay attention. Men act out when they feel threatened or insecure. Your husband is a big strong man, but he's still human, Leena," Fidelia said with a soft smile. "Don't make the mistake of believing he's not as vulnerable as you are."

Leena sat in silence for a few moments. "*Ja*, I see what you mean."

She took a deep breath and then jumped at the tap on the front door. Her gaze flew to the clock, and she groaned as she realized she was late opening the bakery. "No more time for chatting," she said as she rose.

Leticia was home with Angus and would not be in to work the front counter. Fidelia rushed to the front with a broad smile as she welcomed in the first customers of the day. Later that morning during a small lull, Fidelia was elbow deep in soap water, and Leena was waiting for apple cakes and *pepperkake* to finish baking in the oven. She heard the front door jingle, and she swiped at her palms as she moved to attend the customer. Her stride hitched as she saw who awaited her. "Good morning, Mrs. Jameson," she said as she clasped her hands in front of her.

"I'm surprised any God-fearing townsfolk are willing to frequent a store with three women of ill repute." She glared at Leena. "Or should I say four?" Mrs. Jameson clung to her bitterness and spite the way a preacher did the Bible. She loathed the MacKinnons and anyone associated with them. First, because none of the MacKinnon brothers had agreed to marry her daughter, Helen. And then because they had befriended her daughter after she had married Warren Clark. Unable to acknowledge the part she had played in her estrangement from Helen, Mrs. Jameson relished lashing out at all who would listen.

Leena stood tall and glared at Mrs. Jameson. "I do not understand what you mean."

"Don't act like an ignorant foreigner when I know you speak English better than I do," she snapped. "The very beginning of it all was the whore's sister tempting a good businessman into marriage by kissing him in public. Then there was that scandalous so-called schoolteacher who bamboozled another fine man into marriage." Mrs. Jameson blinked as though she were trying not to cry at the mention of Leticia marrying Alistair MacKinnon. "Then the town harlot comes to work here, welcomed by all and forgiven by nearly as many." She glared daggers into the kitchen as though able to do Fidelia bodily harm with a stare.

Soon her focus was on a stony Leena. "And now there is you.

Entertaining men in the back room on a stormy night. Did you believe that the blizzard would prevent those of us astute enough to follow the goings-on in town from noticing that you had your lover visit you last night?" Mrs. Jameson smiled with malicious intent as Leena paled. "That you had him sneak out after your bout of passion, with less regard for the morals of this town than the whores at the Boudoir?"

"I think you should leave, Mrs. Jameson. I fear I have nothing to sell you today," Leena said, her words emerging clipped and tinged with anger.

"You're no better than my own daughter," Mrs. Jameson said. "A strumpet who doesn't even know how to keep a man." She gasped as Leena slapped her across the cheek. "This isn't the last you've heard from me." Mrs. Jameson spun and burst out the door, holding her head high and her cheek out, as though to show it off to the townsfolk.

Leena collapsed against the back wall as the fight left her. "What have I done?" she whispered.

Fidelia marched through the room, flipped the sign from *Open* to *Closed* and pushed Leena to the back room. "Keep baking, but don't answer the front or back door. Wait here." She pulled on her coat as she rushed from the room.

Less than ten minutes later, a breathless Fidelia returned with Warren on her heels. He looked at Leena and sniffed the air. "Whatever you are making smells wonderful." Warren Clark, the town lawyer, had married Helen Jameson in February. A tall, lanky man, his brown hair was disheveled as though he had run his hands through it many times while reviewing a legal document, and his bright blue eyes were filled with curiosity as he waited for Leena to explain why he was here.

Leena jumped up from a dazed stupor and pulled her pans of apple cake from the oven. When she had them on the cooling rack, she faced Warren Clark, her shoulders stooped. "I'm in trouble."

Warren motioned for her to sit and for Fidelia to join them. "I imagine you must believe so, or you wouldn't have summoned me."

He waited for Leena to speak as he pulled out a small notepad from his breast pocket along with a pencil.

"Mrs. Jameson visited today and accused me of acting like a … a …" Leena flushed and ducked her head.

"Like a whore," Fidelia said flatly. "She knows Leena had company here last night and accused her of entertaining her lover."

Warren frowned. "Who was here?"

"My husband," Leena whispered. "For a while. Until we fought, and he left."

"And he'll attest to this?" Warren asked. He smiled as Leena blushed. "No need for embarrassment, Leena, if it was your husband. If it were someone else …" He saw her eyes grow wide at the suggestion, and he relaxed. "Good, so Karl was here. You fought. He stormed out, and Mrs. Jameson believes you are entertaining men in the back rooms while blizzards rage and the townsfolk are blissfully unaware." He tapped his pencil on the paper.

Leena nodded, suddenly fighting a smile at his ability to summarize the predicament in such a dry manner.

"I'm still uncertain why you feel you need my help."

Leena ducked her head again as her smile faded. "I slapped her," she blurted out.

Warren raised his eyebrows and nodded. "I see." He fought a smile and failed. "I imagine that felt …" He flushed and concentrated on his sparse notes as he ignored Fidelia's chuckle. "She's a woman who knows how to rile a person." He cleared his throat as he fought saying anything more about his mother-in-law.

Fidelia grinned. "Says the man who has to deal with her frequently."

He nodded. "Too frequently for my taste. Thankfully Helen has the sense not to invite her for dinner." He half smiled as he winked at Leena. "I know Mrs. Jameson will try to imply that you abused her horribly in the bakery. However, Fidelia was present, and it can be shown that it was not in your nature to act in such a way."

Leena frowned. "She muttered about compensation and tax as she left."

"I imagine she believes the townsfolk are due a portion of the prostitute tax, due to the events she believed were occurring in your private rooms." He smiled triumphantly, and Leena stared at him as his smile transformed him into an exceedingly handsome man. "I'd sue her for slander. And claim that you were defending yourself from her defamation of character."

"Could I do that?"

Warren nodded as Fidelia clapped her hands with glee. "Of course. A woman should know better than to attack another woman's reputation. And, when she accuses you of acting in a manner that could lead to the dissolution of your marriage and could hurt your business here at the bakery *and* could cause you the loss of respect in the townsfolk's eyes, you have every right to protect yourself as you see fit." He sighed as he rubbed at his forehead. "I know for a fact it can be hard to get that woman to stop yammering when she gets a harebrained idea."

"Should I speak with Karl first?" Leena whispered.

Warren shrugged. "Since you two are separated, that will take additional time, and right now we have strategy and surprise on our side. If we squander those elements, you will lose some townsfolk support as Mrs. Jameson spreads her vicious gossip."

"What would you suggest, Warren?" Fidelia asked as Leena sat in deep contemplation.

"I would have the town lawyer speak with Mrs. Jameson and inform her that she is to be sued for her actions. And then I'd have the newspaper woman report about it. Tomorrow is a day for the paper, and J.P. is always looking for news, especially in winter."

Leena looked at Warren for a long moment before she sat tall. "*Ja*, I agree. Please do as you suggest." She looked around the bakery. "I don't know when I'll have time today to speak with Mrs. MacKinnon."

Warren winked at Leena as he rose, smiling as he accepted a cooling apple cake from Fidelia. "It'll be J.P.'s pleasure to come speak with you." He paused as he approached the door. "Don't worry, Leena. All will be fine. Bullies rarely know what to do when they are challenged."

Leena watched Warren leave and then rose to pull out the *pepperkake* from the oven.

Fidelia sighed and rose too, pausing before entering the front room to flick the sign to *Open*. "This will be one day Annabelle is sorry to have missed working." Fidelia shared a rueful smile with Leena before settling behind the counter in the front room.

CHAPTER 6

The next morning Leena entered the General Store—or the Merc, as the townsfolk called it—with a jingle of the bell hanging over the door. An empty basket swung on her elbow. Although now two general stores were in Bear Grass Springs, only Tobias Sutton, who owned the Merc, had reliably ordered the spices Leena required for her baking. Tall windows on either side of the glass door allowed whatever dim light from the cloud-covered day to enter the store. Lamps along the walls enhanced nooks and crannies jammed full of household necessities and farming equipment, lending the store a mysterious air.

Tobias emerged from the back and smirked at Leena. Although Irene and Harold Tompkins were his aunt and uncle, Tobias had none of their charm or compassion. "Well, if it isn't the latest strumpet to call the bakery home."

She stiffened, her back going straighter as she met his derisive gaze. "I have done nothing I am ashamed of."

He snorted as his eyes danced with malicious glee. "Do you think the townsfolk will remain eager to purchase *any* goods from you? Never mind Christmas goods?" He leaned forward as though imparting a secret. "Christmas is a time of family, charity and remembering what is holy. No one will want your treats to sully their home or their Christmas table, unless they're served at the Boudoir."

Leena blushed beet red as she glared at Tobias. "*Ja*, Christmas is a time of family. It is also a time to remember what should be cherished. Trust. Honor. Respect." She watched him curiously as her words affected him.

"Your spices are here, but I find that they're more expensive than the last shipment." He quoted a price three times higher than their arranged price.

Leena blanched and then nodded. "I feared you would act in this manner. So did Jessamine." She waited as Tobias stilled. "You are too friendly with those who should be avoided and relish listening to their gossip."

"Nothing you say will change the price of your spices." He smiled as though he had the upper hand. He seemed to take joy in his ability to threaten her business.

"I hope you will see reason and keep the previously arranged price so that Jessamine does not feel a need to publish an exposé on you." Leena sighed and shrugged. "Although she has it prepared and ready to print at a moment's notice."

Tobias paled and then flushed a crimson red. "That's despicable. How dare she?"

Leena firmed her shoulders and stepped all the way up to the counter, placing her basket on it. "How dare you threaten me when all you know is gossip, not fact? What do you believe would happen to your store when the truth is known about you?"

He glared and spun to his back room. A few minutes later he emerged with smalls sacks of spices for Leena. "Fine. I agree to our original terms. But I won't forget this."

Leena met his glare. "Neither will I." She placed her parcels in her basket and marched out of his store with a triumphant air.

~

Karl poked his head into the sawmill's small office, frowning to see Nathanial sitting, staring into space. "Nathanial?" He spoke to him in Norwegian as they were the only ones around. A tiny window let in the day's weak sunlight, and a small potbellied stove kept the room warm.

Nathanial turned to stare at Karl and frowned. "Why are you here? I thought you were moving to Butte."

Karl flushed and walked into the office area with a hesitant step. "No. I realize that would only make me more of a fool." He sat in his customary chair on the other side of Nathanial's large desk, where they had spent so many hours together doing paperwork, hammering out ideas for expansions and the correct prices for their lumber.

His friend stared at him and then gave a grunt of agreement. "*Ja.* What are you going to do?"

Karl shook his head. "I don't know, but I know I want Leena back. Somehow Leena and I will find our peace." He frowned as his friend flushed. "What is it, Nathanial? Have you found a new partner?"

Nathanial glared at him. "No, you are my partner, even if you have been acting like a fool. I had hoped we would settle this before the busy season started again." He shook his head. "I heard a rumor when I was in town this morning. That Leena ..."

Karl canted forward, his gaze desperate and intense as his friend broke eye contact and ducked his head as though ashamed. "What about Leena? Is she ill? Is she leaving town? Has she ..." His voice broke. "Has she found another?"

Nathanial's eyes flashed with regret at the last question. "Leena had a visitor a few nights ago. Late at night." His tortured gaze met Karl's. "I ..." He frowned as Karl grinned and then laughed.

"That was me," Karl said as he leaned back in his chair and sighed with relief. "*Me.*"

Nathanial grinned at his friend and relaxed into his chair. He rubbed a hand through his blond hair and then laughed. "Thank God. I feared ... I feared you had waited too long." He frowned. "But it didn't sound like Leena. I know she has been angry with you, but I also know she loves you."

Karl's delight dimmed at his friend's words. "I hope what you say is true." He paused. "Somehow I have to show her that I am the man she still wants."

~

That evening Karl sat at the café and listened to the townsfolk murmur. He had attempted to ignore the fact that their chatter came to an abrupt halt when he entered and then restarted in low whispers that could not be overheard when he sat. He sighed and picked up the newspaper on the table as he awaited his meal. He choked on his coffee as he read the prominent story of the day.

News and Noteworthy

It has come to this reporter's attention that a certain resident of this town is insistent on making those around her as miserable as she is. Discontented because her daughter escaped her orbit of influence by marrying the town lawyer, she is intent to ruin or discredit anyone she deems vulnerable.

However, this time, it appears she has met her match. Our newest baker, Mrs. Johansen, is unwilling to suffer Mrs. Jameson's disparaging comments nor is Mrs. Johansen willing to risk her reputation or marriage to Mrs. Jameson's imaginings.

If you are unaware of the details, it appears Mrs. Jameson is so desperate to fabricate gossip that she will wander the streets of our town, even on the night of a blizzard. During such a night, she saw a man visit Mrs. Johansen, who currently resides at the bakery. The following day, without knowing the particulars, Mrs. Jameson accused our respectable baker of partaking in activities made popular by the Boudoir Beauties. Needless to say, Mrs. Johansen was irate at such an accusation as she had had a private dinner with her husband at the bakery after hours.

Mr. Clark, our honorable lawyer, has informed Mrs. Jameson that she will be sued, for an undisclosed amount, for slander. Who, dear reader, are you rooting for?

Karl sat, his mouth agape at the article. He slowly raised his head and stared at the other patrons in the café, who surreptitiously watched him for his reaction. Setting aside the paper, he took another sip of coffee and then tapped his fingers with impatience for Harold to appear. After a few minutes the older man approached Karl's table but without a plate of food.

"I thought you might like to sit in the kitchen," Harold said with a wink. "I saw you reading our day's entertainment."

Karl flushed red and rose, following Harold to the kitchen, where Irene whipped together another batch of biscuits. Karl sat, a bowl of hearty beef stew and a plateful of biscuits slathered in butter in front of him.

"Eat," Irene said. "Everything appears worse on an empty stomach." She swiped her hands on her apron and watched Karl as he sat in stupefied wonder. "Had no idea the lawyer had been summoned, did you?"

Karl shook his head. "Why wouldn't Leena speak to me about something that important?"

Harold sat beside Karl for a moment. "I imagine she has her reasons." He waited until Karl looked at him. "And I wouldn't get notions of not being needed until you hear from her. If Warren was called in, and it sounds like he was, there probably wasn't time to get you involved too."

"I hate this," Karl whispered. After Irene motioned for him to eat, he took a bite of the stew and ate the entire bowl without further comment. He watched as Harold came and went between the kitchen and café, sitting in a stupefied state.

"What do you hate, Karl?" Irene asked. She sat with a groan to finally be off her feet after so many hours working.

"Being the center of the town's gossip. That Leena was shamed for no reason." He shook his head and stared at the kind woman who acted as an aunt to those close to her.

"Speak to your wife, Karl. I imagine she is worried about how you are reacting after reading the paper."

He rose and nodded his thanks for the meal. "Thank you, Mrs. Tompkins."

She squeezed his arm as he moved past her and then exited the café's front door. When he stood on the boardwalk, he paused a moment before walking the short distance to the bakery. The curtains were drawn, and no lights were on in the front part of the bakery. He knocked on the front door, holding little hope that Leena would answer it. Just as he was about to find a way through the snowdrifts to the back door, he saw a light flickering inside the bakery.

"Leena, it's Karl," he called out in Norwegian. He held his breath until he heard the lock *click*, and the door eased open. "Hello, love."

"Karl," she breathed and then shivered as cold air entered the storefront. She stepped back to allow him to enter. "I ... I thought you might visit."

He nodded. "*Ja*, when you are the center of the town's gossip."

She stiffened and thrust back her shoulders. "I have done nothing wrong."

He stilled, watching as a mantle of defiance and despair clung to her. "No, you haven't. But I want to hear from you, my wife, what really happened." He waited as she watched him guardedly. "I want to know why you had to act with such speed that you couldn't speak with me first, *ja*?"

She nodded and then motioned for him to follow her to the warm kitchen where the ovens still pumped out heat. She stilled as he grasped her shoulders and massaged them for a few minutes, easing some of her tension. "Heaven," she whispered as she leaned back into him.

"What did that woman say, Leena?" Karl asked as she sat on a stool next to him. He held onto her hand, refusing to sever all connection with her.

"She accused me of entertaining men in the back room. Of acting no better than a woman who works at the … at the …" She tilted her head to the side in the direction of the Boudoir.

"She called you a prostitute?" Karl roared. He stood, his hands forming fists as though ready for battle.

She jumped to her feet, running soothing strokes over his shoulders and arms in an attempt to calm him. "It's all right, Karl."

"How can you say that her calling you such a thing is all right?" He breathed deeply as though he had just run a mile. "That woman should be horsewhipped for speaking about you in such a manner." He calmed as he saw his wife bow her head, and he watched her curiously because he was uncertain if she felt shame or pride.

"Leena?" he whispered, tilting her chin toward him with two fingers so she would meet his gaze.

"I slapped her," she said with a defiant lift of her chin. "And she ceased her accusations." At the pride shining in his eyes, her smile bloomed. "However, I never meant to act like that. I've never hit anyone before."

"Why, Leena, do you worry about standing up for yourself, when you knew she spoke lies?"

"She was trying to sully the time I had spent with you. Precious time. And, in that moment, I hated her for it." She saw his gaze soften, and she blinked away tears. "I wanted to speak with you before I had Warren approach her and before I spoke with Jessamine, but Warren and Fidelia insisted I needed to act quickly to prevent Mrs. Jameson's vicious rumors from spreading and sticking."

Karl nodded, his gaze guarded but hopeful. "But you did want to speak with me first?"

"Yes," she whispered. "I wasn't sure if I was doing the right thing. I hoped I was. Everything would have been easier if you were by my side."

He groaned and pulled her to him, holding her close. "Oh, my love," he rasped, holding her tightly. "When I read the article in the café, I was afraid that it meant you didn't need me anymore. That you were strong enough without me."

Leena rubbed her face against his chest and then pushed away. "I am strong, Karl. Most women are. But that doesn't mean I don't need you." She sighed and pushed herself into his embrace again.

"*Jeg elsker deg,* Leena," Karl whispered. He held his breath as he waited for her to speak.

"Oh, Karl," she sighed. She arched up on her toes and kissed his jaw and then his cheek. "*Jeg elsker deg.* I love you. I love you so much."

He groaned and hauled her closer. "Come home with me. Make a life with me," he gasped as he rained kisses over her face and neck. He stilled as he tasted the salt of her tears. "Leena?" His callused fingers swiped away her tears. "Why are you crying?"

"Nothing is settled between us. You tempt me with coming home, but …" She shook her head as tears coursed out. "I still want this life." She held out her arms to showcase the bakery.

He nodded and looked around as though seeing it for the first time. "Come." He gripped her hand and tugged her into the adjacent sitting room. He watched as she settled on the rocking chair, and he pulled out the desk chair, to sit facing her and close enough to touch her knee or reach for her hand. "Will you tell me about the bakery?"

Her eyes widened at his question. "You've never wanted to know," she whispered.

"*Ja,* 'tis true. I want to now." He waited as she stared deeply into his shining blue eyes. "Help me understand, my love."

She took a deep breath, and soon her hesitant voice was strong and filled with passion, humor and joy as she spoke about working with Annabelle, Fidelia, Sorcha and Leticia. Leena's voice rang with pride as she said, "I knew the townsfolk would like my *pepperkake,* but I never thought I'd sell out in less than two hours. Now I make twice as much each day but still sell out just as quickly."

"How often do you bake it?" he asked as he watched her with a distant expression.

"Only twice a week. Leticia, who has a great mind for business, thought it would be better if it were more of a specialty item." Leena smiled impishly. "However, I change the days so the townsfolk come in each day to ensure they haven't missed it, and they wind up buying apple cake or other treats." Her smile dimmed as Karl failed to celebrate her baking victory. "Next week I will bake the Christmas *julekake* that have been preordered."

"What else do you have planned for the townsfolk?" he asked in a low voice as he listened to her speak about the gingerbread and the Norwegian Christmas cakes she would sell.

"I'm baking a *pepperkake* house to be auctioned off at the New Year's Eve Dance."

He frowned. "You should serve *glogg* with it," he said. "The warm, spicy drink would be a nice change from the sweet punch."

She flushed. "I've never made a good *glogg*."

His smile bloomed, causing her breath to catch. "Then you are fortunate to have married an expert *glogg*-maker." He frowned. "I hope you have the spices I need."

"We can improvise," she whispered, suddenly shy.

He sighed and reached for her hand, his fingers playing with hers. "Leena, thank you for telling me about the bakery. For sharing with me how much you love it." He waited for her to meet his gaze and nod. "I ... I've been jealous."

She stared deeply into his sincere gaze for a long moment. "I never meant to make you feel second best."

"You didn't. My own imaginings did." He frowned. "I'm an orphan, *ja?*" He saw her eyes cloud with sadness as she nodded. "I don't know if my parents died or didn't want me. But I know the Johansens never wanted me."

"I want you," she whispered.

He looked deeply into her eyes as some of his tension eased. "As I want you." He took a deep breath. "I've tried to listen and learn after you left our house. I don't want to spend Christmas alone." His grip tightened on her fingers as she pulled back on her hand. "I don't want to be alone ever again."

"Karl," she whispered, her voice breaking.

"Please, listen." He met her gaze, pleading and desperation deep within his gaze. "I understand your desire to bake as you have until Christmas. From what you've told me, you've made our treats sought after here in Bear Grass Springs." His eyes shone as he looked at her.

"I'm so proud of you, Leena." He frowned as tears coursed down her cheeks. "But I want things to change after the holiday."

"I won't stop working here," she said with a mutinous tilt to her chin. "No gentle words will hinder me!"

He knelt at her side, gripping her arms to hold her from bolting from him. "Listen, please." When she had settled, he spoke in a soft voice. "I've listened. To you. To your friends. And I hope I've learned." He let out a deep breath. "I still want you home, Leena, but not every day."

She shook her head. "I don't understand what you mean."

"*Ja*, I know." He smiled as he looked deeply into her eyes. "I spoke with Fidelia after I left here the other night. She said that you work here alone some days. When Annabelle is caring for her daughter."

Leena nodded and frowned.

"Why does the bakery need two bakers every day?"

"It doesn't. Fridays and Saturdays are our busiest days, and that is when we are both here."

He relaxed his hands, stroking them down her arms. "Then why must you be here every day? Can you and Annabelle split the week?" He smiled. "You work Monday, Wednesday, Friday and Saturday, and she work Tuesday, Thursday, Friday and Saturday. Or the other way around?"

Her mouth open and closed as she gaped at him, speechless.

"Leena?" he whispered. When she remained quiet, he rose and paced away. "Dammit, I'm trying. What more do you want?"

She rose and grabbed his muscled arm. "Karl?" Her eyes were filled with a luminous, wondrous joy as she beheld him. "You would compromise?"

His passion-filled gaze bore into her. "I've come to realize there is little I wouldn't do to reconcile with you, Leena. And I can't bear to take away what brings you joy." He paused as he looked at her, taking in her arched eyebrows, rounded cheekbones and full lips. He caressed a thumb over her jaw, marveling that such a woman was his wife. "I read that newspaperwoman's article on you. Last night."

Leena frowned in confusion.

"The *True and Tantalizing* piece." He took a deep breath and rasped, meeting her gaze with embarrassment. "And I finally understood that baking, here with these women, eases the ache of leaving your mother and sisters behind."

She nodded as tears coursed down her cheeks. "*Ja.*"

"Forgive me for being too stubborn to realize that before."

"Oh, my love," she gasped as she threw herself into his arms. She clung to him as she sobbed.

"*Shh*, love, there is no reason for tears," he murmured as he kissed her head.

"I thought … I thought when you left last time that I'd never get you back. That you'd find a more malleable woman," she hiccuped out.

"Never," he whispered as he cupped her sodden cheeks between his large palms. "Never, my Leena. I want you and only you. From the moment I saw you in Norway, in your mother's kitchen, wearing a blue-and-red apron, I've wanted you."

"Truly?" she whispered. "You never paid me any attention."

He smiled. "I always knew where you were. Your constant touches to my shoulder were a torment."

She shook her head in wonder as she stared at him. "I thought you only wanted to marry me because of the sawmill. Because of your partnership with Nathanial."

He growled and swooped forward to kiss her. "Damn the partnership. Damn the sawmill. I've always wanted *you*, Leena." He sighed, resting his forehead against her. "And the thought that you didn't want me, that you wished you'd married another …" He closed his eyes.

She cupped his cheeks, her fingers moving through his stubble. "I always wanted you too. My only fear was that you didn't want me as I truly am. I'm not going to change, Karl. Not in any essential way."

"Do you want to have a home with me? Do you want our *spedbarn?*"

Her eyes filled with tears at the Norwegian word for children as her lips followed her fingers, peppering his face with kisses. "Yes. I only left our home because I felt I had no other choice. I never wanted to leave you." She met his hopeful gaze. "I haven't slept well without you by my side."

He let out a deep breath and kissed her. "I missed you, every second of every day," he whispered.

"And I you," she said as a sob burst forth.

He pulled her close as he held her, rocking her as she cried. When she quieted, he whispered, "Leena?"

"Don't let your fears turn you into a bully again. I don't know if our marriage could handle it." She relaxed in his embrace as he nodded, tucking her head onto his shoulder and under his chin.

"I will do my best to always share my fears with you, my love," he whispered into her ear.

"And share your love with me too," she said as she kissed his neck.

He groaned and pulled back, kissing her passionately. "I want you home," he rasped.

"Tomorrow," she gasped as his hands loosened her dress and eased her corset free. "For tonight, let us enjoy our time here."

After their lovemaking, Karl ran his hands over his wife's shoulder to her arm and hip and then back up again, leaning forward frequently to give her little kisses. "I've missed this."

"This quiet contentment," she whispered.

"*Ja.*" He leaned forward, breathing in her scent and then wrapped an arm over her waist as he tugged her backside into his front. "I've missed holding you, knowing that I would wake each morning with you in my arms."

"I've missed so much more than that." She grabbed his hand and raised it to her mouth, kissing it. "I missed talking over problems with you, hearing about your day. Reminiscing about Norway. Dreaming about our future."

"Have you enjoyed living in town? Would you rather live closer to the bakery than near the sawmill?"

She pushed against him until she faced him. "No, Karl. I want to live in our home. Near Nathanial. Away from those who love to gossip."

He frowned as he saw her battle anger and embarrassment. "You have loyal friends who will continue to defend you, *min kjærlighet.*"

"The MacKinnons are your friends too," she whispered, kissing him softly.

"What happened to put such shadows in your eyes?" His finger traced under her eye, and his frown deepened.

"I had an argument with Mr. Sutton at the Merc. He wanted to charge me more because he believed I was a woman of loose morals." She gripped his arm as she felt him stiffen with rage next to her.

After a moment he exhaled and relaxed next to her. "How did you persuade him to change his mind?"

She flushed. "Jessamine knows something about his past and advised me what to say to make it seem as though I knew it too. He was terrified for the townsfolk to know whatever he had done." She ducked her head. "I am ashamed I tricked him and used something he is not proud of against him."

Karl growled and tilted her chin so that she would meet his gaze. "He was willing to shame you for something you did not do. He willingly believed the worst about you. I have no sympathy for him."

She sniffled. "That is what Jessamine said."

Karl's gaze shone with pride as he stared at his wife. "Knowledge is power," he whispered. "Thank God you had the newspaperwoman on your side."

Leena giggled as she fell forward into his arms. "She was disappointed Tobias saw sense and relented from charging me an exorbitant amount. I think she is waiting for the day she can expose whatever it is he did."

Karl held Leena close, kissing the top of her head. "I wouldn't be so certain. Once it is divulged, she will have no leverage over him. And, whatever it is, it might hurt those she cares about."

Leena sighed, her fingers playing over his chest muscles. "Stay the night with me?" When he remained silent, she scooted away from him, her shoulders stiffening as though trying to deflect his rejection.

When he grabbed her hands and stilled her erratic movements, she met his tender gaze. "Love, nothing could force me to leave you tonight."

She sighed with happiness and snuggled into the bedcovers with him again.

～

"Leena, love, wake up," Karl whispered as he kissed her shoulder. She snuggled into his embrace. "No," she murmured as she shivered at his touch. "Don't make me."

"Come, love. You have work to do." He kissed her again and pulled his arm from around her waist. He stopped moving when she gripped his arm, her fingernails biting into his muscles.

"Karl?" she breathed, releasing him and turning over to see him. She traced a finger over his arm and then his face. "You're really here? This wasn't a dream?"

He smiled at her, a relieved sigh escaping as he kissed her. "I'm here. If I am lucky, I will spend every night beside you." His smile turned mischievous. "However, Annabelle will find me in your bed if you don't get up soon."

Leena beamed at him. "Let her find you here. She's only ever wanted us to find happiness, Karl. She never meant to cause strife between us by offering me a place to stay."

He pulled his wife close, breathing in her scent. He jerked when he heard the back door open and slam shut, Annabelle's voice calling out for Leena. He tugged the blankets up over her to ensure they were covered to their chins and then looked toward the door with an amused expression.

Annabelle entered the back room with a lantern, one hand absently tucking errant strands of hair into her bun. She stilled when she met Karl's gaze. "Oh, I beg your pardon," she whispered. "I … I'll see you when you—" She spun on her heels and slammed the bedroom door shut behind her.

Leena groaned while Karl burst into laughter. "I've never seen your friend, who is so composed and in command, at a loss for words before."

"It's the first shocking thing I've ever done." Leena kissed his neck and sighed as she prepared herself for rising in the cold room.

He eased her down into the bed and crawled over her, moving to the small stove to rekindle the embers and to add wood. "Wait a few minutes to allow the room to warm. Then you can prepare your delicacies to share with the townsfolk." He crawled back into bed with her, sighing with pleasure as she plastered herself along his front.

"You can stay here for as long as you want, darling. However, there will be more noise once Fidelia and Leticia arrive."

He kissed her head. "I'll sleep a while longer before traveling home." After a few minutes, he reluctantly opened his arms so she could ease out of them to dress for the day. He closed his eyes with blissful tenderness when she kissed his forehead and then his lips before venturing into the kitchen area to cook.

Although he remained in bed, he did not sleep. He listened to the women's voices, their camaraderie as they told stories and laughed. He could not make out what they said, but their affection and friendship was evident. After a few hours, two new voices joined in, and he knew it was time to rise.

He dressed and eased open the sitting room door, stilling his movements as he beheld Leena. Her apron was covered in flour; she had a streak of something marring one cheek, and her hands were elbow deep in a bowl, kneading bread. She giggled at something Leticia said, and his breath caught at her joy.

For a moment he was transported back to her mother's house in Norway, where Leena had spent so many hours in the kitchen. So often she had looked just like this, with joy and laughter pervading her as she had chatted with her sisters and mother. Suddenly he understood that she had recreated what she had lost by moving to

America. She had a place that was like home, with women who were like family to her.

His throat tightened at the thought of what he had attempted to deprive her of, and he cleared his throat. The gruff sound alerted the women to his presence, and their chattering halted.

Leena glanced at him, her smile fading as she saw his serious countenance.

Her eyes rounded as he strode toward her, gripped her shoulders and kissed her soundly. "You belong here, my love. I will pick you up this afternoon." He kissed her again, nodded to the women who watched him with shocked expressions and then marched out the back door.

Fidelia swiped her hands on a towel and then gave Leena a little smack with it. "Well, it seems one of us has something to tell."

Leena flushed but could not hide her contented smile. "*Ja.* Karl read Jessamine's article last night while he was at the café, and he came here to ensure I was fine."

"Seems he made sure you were more than fine," Leticia said with a wry smile, causing Fidelia to snort and Annabelle to laugh.

Annabelle sobered as she studied her friend. "Does this mean you are moving home?"

Leena looked at all of them, noting how Fidelia tensed. "*Ja.* Karl listened to why I love working here. He understands. He no longer resents it."

Fidelia relaxed and smiled at her friend. "Your gamble paid off."

Annabelle gave Leena a hug, unconcerned about Leena's flour-stained apron. "I'm so happy, Leena. You were never meant to live here."

Leena nodded as she pulled back from Annabelle. "Thank you for giving me the space I needed to see the strength I have. And for Karl to come to understand that we must compromise in this marriage." She took a deep breath. "As we must compromise in the bakery."

Annabelle frowned. "I don't understand." She sat on a stool as Leena gripped her fingers together.

"Karl understands my desire to work here, but he does not want me to work here every day. He learned that there are days you are absent, and he believes we should have a schedule where we each work the bakery alone two days a week, and then on Friday and Saturday we work it together."

Annabelle frowned as she cast a look at her sister, who shrugged. "So his plan would be that we share the duties?"

Leena bit her lip. "*Ja.*"

Annabelle sighed and rubbed at her head. "That seems only fair to me. I fear I have taken advantage of the fact you are here so I can spend more time at home with Skye. Having a schedule would be good for both of us." She met Leena's relieved gaze. "And I will do what I must so that I don't lose you, Leena. Not just because you are a brilliant baker but because of your friendship. Our little shop wouldn't be the same without you."

Fidelia gave a nod of agreement as Leena swiped at tears. "Thank you." Annabelle gave her another quick hug before they washed their hands and resumed baking for the day.

That afternoon Ewan slipped into the printing shop that his wife ran, heating his hands over the warm potbellied stove in the center of the room. The number of excess papers had been drastically reduced in the recent weeks as she had burned them for heat. Thus there was now room near the entrance, and the space appeared twice as large as when he had first entered her printing shop fifteen months ago.

He frowned as he heard sniffling. "Jessie?" he called out as he flipped the lock on the front door. He wandered around to the back area of the room where she still had a small cot. He frowned as he saw her perched on it, tears coursing down her cheeks. "Oh, my love, what is it?" He knelt in front of her and clasped her hands. "Yer article was a triumph."

"Why aren't you at work?" she whispered in frustration as she tugged at one of her hands. When he wouldn't free her hands but instead held both of hers with one of his and swiped at her cheeks with his callused fingers, she leaned forward and buried her face in his neck.

"Come, love. Share with me whatever has caused this sorrow. I'll make it better. I promise."

She sobbed and clung to him. "You can't," she stammered out. After a few moments, her crying calmed, and she relaxed in his hold. He pushed her onto the cot and joined her, kicking off his boots.

"'Tis like when we first met, afore we were married," he said with a smile as he tugged her to him, chest to chest, with her face buried in his neck.

"I've failed you, Ewan," she whispered.

He jerked back and shook his head. "*Nae*, ye never could, Jessie." He stroked thumbs over her cheeks and then kissed each eyebrow. "What is it, darling?"

"I spoke with Helen a few months ago." She made a shushing noise as she saw the delight and hope flare in his gaze. Fat tears formed and tracked down her cheeks. "She thought I was pregnant. I'm not. I … I have my courses again today." She met his saddened gaze as tears continued to pour down her cheeks. "I … I thought this would be my Christmas surprise for you."

"Oh, love." He kissed her forehead. "We'll keep trying, aye?" he whispered. "Not having a bairn doesna make ye a failure."

"You're going to want what your brothers have!" She stopped speaking as he pushed her so he leaned over her, his countenance irate.

"Aye, an' I do, ye ken? I have ye, the woman I love. The woman I want with me until the day I die." He gripped her head between his strong palms. "If we dinna have a bairn, I'll be all right because I still have *ye*, Jessie. As long as I have ye, I'll never want for anythin' more."

She nodded and curled into his arms, her hold on him as fierce as his on hers.

"Are ye sure ye were pregnant?" he whispered after many minutes of holding her.

"I ... I don't know. I think so."

"Talk with Helen, darling, to help with yer doubts." He kissed her head and tugged her even closer into his embrace.

"I love you, Ewan," she whispered.

"An' I ye, Jessie."

CHAPTER 7

On the twenty-third of December, Leena gave Annabelle, Leticia and Fidelia hugs before she wrapped herself in her warm outerwear as she prepared for the sleigh ride home. She carried a basket filled with goodies outside and smiled at Karl as he grabbed the basket from her. He stowed it in the sleigh before helping her into the seat. After bundling under the blanket, she snuggled into his side. She felt the townsfolk's curious stares as they continued to watch them with fascination after their reconciliation.

"I hope you had a good day, love," Karl whispered as he gave a *click* to the horse. The sleigh seemed to move effortlessly as they sped past the livery, church and school. He chuckled as he felt her relax the farther they traveled from town. "I thought you liked working at the bakery."

She squeezed his arm at the teasing. "*Ja*, you know I do. But I'm looking forward to the break. To time away from the gossips." She sighed as she rested her head against his arm. "The townsfolk are fascinated by my disagreement with Mrs. Jameson."

"*Our* argument too," he muttered.

She smiled and stroked a hand down his arm. After a moment she sighed in pleasure. "I'm looking forward to my time with my husband.

Four days for us." She felt him tense next to her and frowned. "What is it?"

"I agreed to go to Cailean MacKinnon's house for Christmas dinner. I thought you would be pleased." He glanced down at her, worry marring his bright blue eyes.

She sighed. "I am, and I know Nathanial will enjoy being with his friends." She leaned into his side. "I was being selfish."

"No," he teased. "You were acting like a newly married wife."

She blushed and giggled but did not disagree with him.

"I have a surprise for you at home, my love," he whispered, kissing her forehead.

When they arrived at their small house, Nathanial walked over from his house and took the horse and sleigh to the barn. "Thank you, Nathanial," Karl said, running a gloved finger over the furrow between his wife's eyebrows. "He is ensuring my surprise is not ruined."

She giggled at her husband's teasing tone and kissed him. "Should I close my eyes?"

"Excellent idea." He put his hands on her shoulders and steered her inside. When the door closed, he whispered, "You can open them now."

She gasped as she saw the small tree, standing in the living room area, with paper decorations on it in heart-shaped baskets. "Oh, Karl," she rasped as she turned and flung herself into his arms, holding him close.

"This is our first Christmas together, Leena. I cannot buy you jewels or fancy clothes—"

She put her hand over his lips. "*Shh*, none of that. I have a home with you. I need none of those things that do not prove love or devotion. Those are just things, Karl." She turned to look at the tree. "It must have taken you hours to cut out all the decorations."

He flushed as she looked at him with love and wonder. "*Ja*, but there is not much work at the sawmill just now." He kissed her softly. "I love you, my Leena. I know you miss home."

She shook her head and traced his eyebrows that had risen in surprise at her denial. "I miss Norway, but here, with you, is home, Karl."

He cupped her cheeks with his strong hands and held her face tenderly. "I want our home to always be where you want to be."

Her eyes glowed with love and the promise of their future. "It is. It always will be." She leaned forward to meet his kiss. Their hands tangled as they fought buttons and knotted strings, and she giggled. "I hope we never lose this."

His eyes shone with devotion and passion. "We won't, *min kjærlighet.*" He held out his hand and tugged her toward their bed. "Come, my love," he whispered. "Dinner can wait."

The following afternoon Leena spun toward the door as it opened, beaming at her husband and brother as they entered her house. She had pulled the small table away from the wall, then covered it with a red tablecloth, and a candle sat ready to be lit as they celebrated their Christmas Eve festivities. Karl kissed her cheek, and Nathanial gave her a hug. She shivered from the cold as they had come from the barn and had tended the animals for the evening. "Whatever you are cooking smells heavenly," Karl said as he sat with a contented sigh.

"*Ja,*" Nathanial agreed. "Although we should have had this celebration at my house. It's much larger."

"No," Leena said as she set a hand on her husband's shoulder. "This is our first Christmas together, and Karl and I wanted to celebrate in our home."

Nathanial studied his sister and his best friend before nodding as he sensed the harmony between them. "*God Jul!*"

Leena clapped her hands with joy and then moved to the stove to ladle out warm mugs of *glogg.* "Karl made this. I think it tastes delicious, and I hope we can share it with the townsfolk next week at the New Year's Eve Dance." She waited as her brother took a sip and frowned as he made a sour face. Her grip on her husband's shoulder tightened as Karl tensed.

"You plan on giving this to them?" Nathanial asked.

Karl nodded, his shoulders tightening further.

"Fool. You should charge for it." Nathanial smiled at his friend and laughed. "I've never tasted a better *glogg*."

Leena's breath *whoosh*ed out of her as she realized her brother had been teasing Karl and then laughed. "Oh, it's like old times," she whispered as she swiped at her eyes. She met her brother's smile and then shrieked as Karl tugged her to sit on his lap. "Where you take great joy in tormenting each other."

"All in good fun," Karl said with a sigh as he nuzzled the side of her neck.

After a moment Leena pushed up and moved to the stove. "Isn't this the most marvelous stove? Karl bought it just for me." She beamed at her husband with pride and happiness at his thoughtful purchase. She opened the oven door and pulled out a tray of braised pork ribs, placing it on top of the stove. After extracting potatoes and finely chopped cabbage cooked with caraway seeds and vinegar, she plated them each a portion. After serving her brother and husband, she sat.

"I will always miss the *lutefisk*," Karl said as he recalled the tenderized and cured cod that was a specialty eaten during the holidays in Norway. He gripped his wife's hand a moment. "Thank you for making us our special foods, Leena."

Nathanial nodded. "*Ja*, tomorrow will be a nice day with the MacKinnons, but it is good to have time to remember our ways."

Leena smiled. "You're welcome. I don't want to forget either. And this helps me feel closer to those who are so far away."

After they had eaten their meal, as she rose to fix a pot of coffee and to serve dessert, she asked, "Did you leave the *risengrynsgrøt* in the barn?"

Karl nodded and gripped her hand. "Of course. Any gnome that finds it will be delighted." He winked at his wife.

"I know you think me foolish, but I want us to continue to have good fortune." She flushed as she thought of what her friends and neighbors would think should they realize they had left a bowl of delicious rice pudding in the barn.

"It is an important tradition to you, my love. It does not matter what others think," Karl said as he squeezed her hand.

"As long as you kept plenty for us," Nathanial joked. "It's my favorite holiday treat." He met his sister's challenging look. "Well, except for your *pepperkake*."

Leena smiled. "I baked *pepperkake* today too." She laughed at Nathanial's *whoop* of delight. "You can't eat it all, Nathanial, like you did when you were fifteen. We must bring some to the MacKinnons tomorrow." She smiled as Karl watched them with curiosity. "You don't remember, do you? You were never at our house for the holiday season."

Karl's delight dimmed as his smile faded. "I was forbidden from visiting you and your family at that time. I was told I was not to pester your family."

"Oh, Karl," Leena said as she gripped his hand. "If you only knew how many times our mother looked to the door, as though awaiting your arrival. We always had a place set for you."

Nathanial nodded. "*Ja,* I think that was Leena's doing. I should have known she was sweet on you from the beginning. It was not only our mother staring at the door like a lost calf." He sat back in his chair and kicked out his legs to the side as he sighed after eating his fill of the delicious meal. "The Johansens were miserable people, Karl. Nothing they said was true."

Karl cleared his throat as he looked from his wife to his best friend. "You wanted me there?" At their nods, he took a deep, stuttering breath.

"Always," Leena whispered, running her hand over the back of his head and nape, kissing him softly on his forehead. "Always, my love."

～

L ater that evening Leena brushed and braided her hair before crawling into bed. Karl insisted she sleep on the side toward the stove so that she had more warmth. "Merry Christmas, my love," she whispered.

He groaned and wrapped his arms around her, pulling her close. "Merry Christmas, Leena." He took a deep breath and shuddered as though battling deep emotions.

"What is it?" She ran fingers over his cheeks and frowned to find them wet. "Why are you crying?"

He shook his head and pulled her closer. After many minutes he let out a deep breath and relaxed in her embrace. "Do you know, … do you know, my Leena, what it means to be here with you? To have your arms around me? To know of your steadfast devotion for years?" He shook his head as though words failed him.

She moved so that she freed herself from his hold and cupped his face. "*Min kjærlighet*, my love, my beloved husband." She paused as she kissed him. "You are the only man I have ever seen. The only one I have ever wanted. Nothing they ever said about you is true." She let go of his face and tugged his hand, holding it to her heart. "The truth of you is etched in my heart, as mine is etched in yours."

He looked deeply into her eyes. "What is that truth?"

"You are a good, strong, stubborn man. You are loyal. You are kind." She smiled as a tear leaked out. "Your stubbornness and pride almost cost us so much, but you were able to acknowledge when you were wrong." She cast a quick look over her shoulder at their small house. "You worked to ensure I felt at home here on our first Christmas together." She kissed him again. "I love you, more than you will ever know."

"Oh, Leena," he rasped as he tugged her close. "Thank you. For forcing me to see that I was being an obstinate fool and hurting you in the process. For enriching my life by bringing the MacKinnons into it." He pressed his forehead against hers. "But most of all, for loving me. *Me.*"

"You have always been worthy of love, my Karl." She leaned forward, kissing him, and soon she was lost to their shared passion.

The following day Leena, Karl and Nathanial traveled to Cailean MacKinnon's house for a Christmas Day dinner and celebration. They entered the small living area, already filled with family and friends. Harold and Irene sat on the settee while Leticia and Annabelle sat near them with their children in their arms. Cailean and Alistair filled glasses with beer from a keg Ewan had smuggled from the Stumble-Out, and Hortence sat beside Bears as he told her stories. Warren and Helen whispered to each other as they admired the tree in the front window.

After exchanging hellos, Leena asked, "Where is Fidelia?"

"In the kitchen," Bears said.

Annabelle smiled at Leena. "She is making sure everything is coming along with the meal." She shook her head as she anticipated Leena's next question. "And, no, there is nothing you can do but relax and enjoy yourself."

Karl tucked her into his side and chuckled as his wife bristled at not being allowed in the kitchen.

"How is Sorcha, Irene?" Leticia asked as she rocked Angus in her arms. She smiled up at her husband, Alistair, as he ran a hand over their son's downy head.

Harold laughed as Irene poked him in his side before she answered Leticia. "Sorcha is fine. It's Frederick you should be worried about. He's going crazy with your sister living there."

"Her jabbering is driving him insane," Harold said.

"No, I think it's because she's shown no interest in him, and he's frustrated," Irene said with an amused smile. "I wish this weather weren't so harsh, or we would have ventured out there to see for ourselves how they got along. As it is, we have to rely on Frederick's letters delivered by ranch hands who travel into town for sporadic visits."

"I don't relish being marooned there," Harold muttered.

"I thought you liked the ranch," Cailean said with a frown.

"I do. I just like town more."

Irene snorted. "He always says I'm the one who will miss the gossip and news we learn at the café when we retire. He'll miss it as much or more than I do!"

They all laughed at Harold's disgruntled expression before filing into the kitchen, where the table had been expanded to accommodate all of them for dinner.

The brothers gathered to one side of the living room after dinner as the women sat and discussed babies, the bakery and Jessamine's recent articles. Cailean noted the tightening of Ewan's jaw as Leticia held Angus high and frowned as Ewan excused himself from the festivities. Cailean motioned for Alistair to stay behind to entertain their guests as he followed his youngest brother.

He found Ewan standing on the back porch, staring vacantly at the piles of snow. "Ewan?" he asked.

"I'm fine, Cail. Ye should be in there enjoyin' yer family and friends," Ewan rasped as he sniffed and turned away.

Cailean's frown deepened. "I was surprised you and Jessamine didn't make an announcement during the family meal today. It would have been the perfect time."

Ewan let out a deep, stuttering breath. "There was no announcement to make," he whispered. "She lost the bairn."

Cailean gripped his shoulder and spun Ewan to face him. He saw the anguish in his brother's eyes a moment before he pulled Ewan close for a bear hug. "Ye'll have another, Ewan. Ye ken that, right?"

"I ken, but it doesna take away the pain. It near ripped out my heart to hold her in my arms as she sobbed. As she said she believed she'd failed me." He pushed away from his brother as his eyes lit with anger. "Why should ye an' Alistair have bairns, an' I be denied?"

Cailean shook his head. "I don't know. Life is rarely fair. Or logical."

Ewan turned and faced the snowy scene again. "I want a child, aye," he whispered as though answering an unspoken question. "But I'll always want Jessie more."

Cailean took a deep breath. "Be sure she understands that. I nearly lost Annabelle after we lost our first bairn. Don't be a fool like I was."

Ewan nodded. "I ... I find it hard to be around the bairns just now. And that makes me a horrible uncle because I do love them."

"No, Ewan, that makes you human," Cailean whispered before spinning to the door as it creaked open. "Hello, Jessamine." He heard his brother sniffle. He squeezed Ewan's shoulder and then slipped inside, leaving Ewan with his wife.

"Why are you hiding from everyone on Christmas? You've always loved Christmas," she whispered. She stroked a hand down his back, eliciting a shudder.

"I needed a moment, Jessie," he whispered.

"I'm sorry to have intruded," she said in a stilted voice. She gasped as he spun and grabbed her wrist, preventing her from returning to the living room. She paled as she saw the anguish and torment in his gaze and the tracks of tears down his cheeks. "Oh, Ewan."

"Hush, love. Dinna cry," he said as he pulled her into his arms. "I ... I needed a moment away from the bairns."

"Away from the reminder of what we won't have," she said as she clung to him.

"*Yet*, my love. We will have children," he said as he eased her away and looked deeply into her eyes. "I meant what I said, Jessie. As long as I have ye, I will be happy. But I've learned I must mourn what I've lost, or I go a little mad." He leaned into her touch as she cupped his cheek. "I love ye so."

"What if I can never have a child?" she asked as she voiced what he suspected was one of her deepest fears.

"Then we'll find another way to have a family." He kissed her palm. "I will love any child we raise together, Jessie. As long as ye are by my side, I will want for nothing more." He looked into her doubtful eyes. "I promise ye."

Her eyes filled, and she stood on her toes to kiss him. "You—you and your love—are my Christmas miracles." She sank into his arms, taking comfort from him as he comforted her.

≈

Karl wandered into the kitchen for another cup of coffee and paused as he saw Annabelle sitting at the table, burping her daughter after feeding her. "I beg your pardon," he said as he flushed and backed out of the room.

She laughed and motioned for him to enter the kitchen. "No, Karl, come in. I wanted a quiet moment with Skye, but she is nearly asleep." She ran a hand over her daughter's head and kissed it before focusing on Karl. "I hope you are well."

He frowned as he stared at her. "I never thought I'd like you. You meddled in my life."

Annabelle flushed and then shrugged. Her hand continued to rub her daughter's back. "I know. However, it's what I do for those I call friend." She paused as she met his searching gaze. "For those I care about."

He moved to the stove, poured himself a cup of coffee and then leaned against the counter as he thought through her words. "You provided Leena with a safe place to live."

"Yes. I could not deny her such a place when I had provided it for myself at one time." She watched surprise flit in his eyes. "Cailean and I had our own share of troubles when we first married." Her smile was filled with sympathetic understanding. "Like you and Leena, we needed time and distance before we could reconcile."

Karl nodded and sipped his coffee. "Thank you." He nodded again at the surprise in her gaze. "Thank you for caring for Leena. For ensuring she was safe." He cleared his throat and swallowed what more he might have said as Cailean entered the kitchen.

"You're welcome, Karl," Annabelle whispered.

He set down his cup, nodded to Cailean and slipped from the room to join the others in the main living area.

~

Leena stood to one side of the sitting room and watched as her husband spoke with Alistair MacKinnon and Bears, Karl's shoulders relaxing as they appeared to tease him. When she heard him laugh, she smiled and glanced around the room. She stiffened when she saw Helen Clark approach her. "Mrs. Clark."

Helen smiled and shook her head. "No need to be formal with me, Leena. I feel as though we are old friends, after hearing Warren speak about you recently." Her wheat-colored hair was pulled back in a tidy chignon, and her cranberry-colored wool dress highlighted her lush figure.

Leena flushed and ducked her head. "I am most embarrassed."

Helen chuckled and shook her head again. "I wouldn't be. I imagine it felt wonderful." She met Leena's shocked gaze. "I spent too many years on the other end of her fist. It is good for her to know what happens when she pushes an honorable woman too far. I fear she believed you were like me."

Leena frowned and shook her head. "I do not understand."

"Malleable. Afraid of a bully." Delight shone in Helen's gaze. "You showed her the error of her assumption."

"You are no longer that person," Leena protested. "I cannot see you allowing her to treat you like that."

Helen's smile softened as she clasped Leena's hand. "You're right, Leena. Since I married Warren, and rarely interact with my mother or brother, my self-respect has grown." She seemed to glow with happiness as her husband approached.

"Are you speaking about the fortunate incident with your mother?" Warren asked.

"Why *fortunate*?" Leena asked.

Warren fought and failed to hide his smile. "Mrs. Jameson is so angry with me for championing you and your *version of events* that she has said she will not acknowledge us for at least a year." He sighed with contentment at the thought. "If only she were a woman of her word."

"Warren!" Helen said with a giggle as she tapped him on his arm.

He shrugged unrepentantly. "I wouldn't mind a few months' reprieve from her natterings."

Leena looked between the pair and smiled. "If I were to win my case against her, I fear she would ostracize you for some time."

"A prayer fulfilled," Warren said while he tipped his head back, as though hoping for such a benediction.

Leena giggled again and shook her head. "Thank you, Mr. Clark, for aiding me. I fear I would have been forced from the bakery had I not taken your advice."

"Oh, I highly doubt that, as Annabelle has a will of iron. However, your acceptance in town might not have been as assured." He smiled. "And it's *Warren* for my friends."

He took a sip of beer and then leaned forward to whisper to her. "As for your case, I have heard that she is willing to rescind what she said as long as you do not require her to pay any monetary damages."

Leena tilted her head to one side and met the lawyer's amused expression. "What do you suggest?"

"I suggest that she write a public apology for the newspaper and be required to donate to the very tax fund she thought you should pay into. That way, the townsfolk will learn that they should not act in such a manner."

"And you'll get the fire equipment the town's Improvement Committee wants that much more rapidly."

"Every little bit helps," Warren said with one raised eyebrow and a shrewd smile.

Leena laughed and looked toward Karl, who watched her with a curious expression. "I must speak with Karl first, and then I will let you know."

Warren nodded, and soon they were enfolded into the larger group as they sang Christmas carols and told Christmas stories.

∽

News and Noteworthy

It has come to this reporter's attention that the one making such slanderous accusations against our honorable baker has been offered a generous reprieve. Rather than be made to suffer further with an injurious court case for any of the harm and anguish she has caused Mrs. Johansen, Mrs. Jameson believes a simple, insincere apology should suffice. However, our esteemed town lawyer believes that only through a show of contrition and sacrifice will Mrs. Jameson truly demonstrate her remorsefulness. And a donation to aid the town's Improvement Committee fund seems little to ask after what she attempted.

What do you think, dear reader?

L eena and Karl walked the short distance from the bakery to the Odd Fellow's Hall for the New Year's Eve Dance. Nathanial would join them there, as would the MacKinnon clan. Karl had helped her transport her large gingerbread house to the Hall, and he had spent a large portion of his day making batches of *glogg* for the evening's revelers. It too was at the Hall, waiting to be served to the guests.

When they entered the Hall, Leena paused with a gasp. "They said they would decorate, but I never imagined such a sight."

Karl squeezed her arm and murmured his agreement.

Paper streamers hung from one rafter to another, and boughs of evergreen lined the windows. A small group of musicians sat to one side, playing music, although no one danced yet. On the far side of the room, a long table was laden with food while Karl's *glogg* sat in a punch bowl next to it. Leena's *pepperkake* house was on a round table to the side of the room, far away from the offered food and desserts.

Soon Leena and Karl stood along one wall, watching the townsfolk interact. "Why are you glaring at those men?" Leena asked as she sipped her husband's perfectly spiced *glogg*.

Karl sent another glower in three miners' direction before focusing on his wife, dressed in a velvet evergreen-hued dress that highlighted her blond hair and blue eyes. "They are a few of the men who commiserated with me about my *errant* wife. Miss Evans helped me to see they were hoping to cause problems between us so that you would leave me, and then one of them would end up with you."

Leena's eyes widened. "I was never interested in any of them. In anyone but you."

"Hush," Karl said with a tender smile as he tugged her free hand up to kiss her palm. "I know, my love. I was too stupid to realize I was being manipulated."

Leena looked deep into his eyes and saw the truth in his gaze, flushing at the love she saw there. After a moment she focused on their friends as the MacKinnons arrived. Annabelle carried Skye in her arms while Leticia held Angus. Hortence raced off to play with friends from school.

"Please tell me that there are gingerbread cookies too, not just that huge cake that we all hope to win," Jessamine said as she hugged Leena.

Leena giggled as she shook her head. "No. If there were cookies, no one would want my *pepperkake* house." She looked with pride at the large gingerbread house, sitting on a table, while Irene and Harold Tompkins acted as guards, lest someone tried to break off a corner piece.

"You heard her, Ewan," Jessamine said with a stroke down her husband's back. "You must be the highest bidder."

Ewan glanced at the large cake. "How do ye plan to eat the whole thing yerself, ye wee demon?" he teased his wife, although a sorrow seemed to cling to him. "Dinna fash," he whispered into her ear as he kissed her on the side of her head.

"It's wonderful to see you here, Fidelia," Leena said as she hugged her friend.

Fidelia relaxed as the townsfolk had barely registered her attendance. This was only the second town function she had attended since escaping the Boudoir thirteen months before. However, her work at the bakery had accustomed the townsfolk to her presence outside of the confines of the Boudoir.

Nathanial joined their group, and they were all together, except for Bears, who never joined the festivities, and Sorcha, who remained at the ranch. Fidelia declined a miner's invitation to dance, moving toward the back of their large group.

"You should dance, Dee," Annabelle said to her sister.

"I already have enough notoriety in this town. I don't want to cause a scene when a man takes liberties."

Cailean frowned. "Some men are respectable and won't take liberties. Someday you will have your faith restored in men."

Fidelia shook her head with doubt at what Cailean said, nodding her thanks as Nathanial handed her a glass of *glogg*. "Oh, this is nice, rather than the sweet punch." She flushed, looking around to ensure she had not offended the woman who made the punch for every town function.

"Karl made it," Leena said with pride. She squeezed his arm as the MacKinnon men pounded him on the back in congratulations. "He also helped me decorate my cake."

"An exemplary husband," Fidelia murmured with a warm smile as she met Leena's gaze.

Jessamine wandered off to scout out a story while the men discussed politics. As Leticia and Annabelle spoke about their children, Leena moved toward Fidelia. "I am sorry your friend Bears is not here."

Fidelia stiffened and then forced herself to relax. "He is everyone's friend, Leena."

Leena frowned and shook her head. "*Ja*, he is friends with everyone. Yet you are the only one he knows where you are at every moment."

"There's nothing between us," Fidelia whispered.

"*Ja*, but it's always good to have a friend," she said as Fidelia's momentary panic seemed to ease.

Fidelia glanced around at their group, noting that the men had moved away and were out of earshot. She and Leena were against the wall, with no one paying any attention to them. "When are you going to tell your husband?"

Leena shook her head in confusion. "I don't know what you mean."

She leaned in and whispered out of habit borne from years of learning to be cautious. "That you are expecting his child."

Leena froze, her eyes going round as she met Fidelia's knowing grin. "I ... I can't be."

"Why can't you be?"

Leena flushed and then gave a tilt of her head. "Of course I can be," she whispered, frowning. She raised her hand as though to put it over her belly and then quickly dropped it. Her eyes filled with wonder as she looked at her friend.

"He will be happy, won't he?" Fidelia asked, unable to hide the concern from her gaze.

"Yes, yes, he will be ... I don't know the word in English."

"*Ecstatic*, I think," Fidelia said as she watched Leena's husband, who frequently glanced in his wife's direction as though to ensure she was well. "He seems a good man, now that you are past your disagreement."

"*Ja*," Leena said as she sniffled. "He always was a good man, but he was afraid."

Fidelia nodded. "And men who are afraid can be irrational."

"Anyone who is afraid can be irrational," Annabelle said as she joined the conversation with Leticia. She glanced around the room and groaned. "Oh, no."

Leena followed her gaze and stiffened as Mrs. Jameson approached their group. Karl noted her arrival and moved to stand beside his wife.

"What do ye want, crone?" Ewan asked as he winked at Jessamine who sidled up next to him.

Mrs. Jameson stiffened at Ewan's insolent tone and then stood tall. "I find it hard to believe that this town has once again forgiven the transgressions of those who should be held in contempt."

Jessamine smiled as she looped her arm through her husband's. "Interesting way you have of apologizing."

Mrs. Jameson turned her glare on Jessamine. "You should have been run out of town. Sent back with your father. Then my daughter would have made a worthy match."

Ewan grinned as he kissed his wife's forehead. "Ye have to ken no MacKinnon would wed yer daughter. An' it wasna because we didna like Helen. It was because we couldna consign ourselves to a life tied to a woman like ye." He sobered as he looked at Mrs. Jameson with disdain. "Besides, Warren would have done us bodily harm."

Mrs. Jameson scoffed. "That man." She glared as she looked around the small group, her glower intensifying as she saw Warren standing beside her daughter and Leena. "That man should know the meaning of family loyalty."

Warren smiled as he placed a calming hand on his wife's shoulder. "I do. I show it every day to my wife." His smile acted as kindling to Mrs. Jameson's ire, and she turned red in the face.

"You should show me as great a consideration. I am like your mother!" She pointed at Leena. "And that woman slapped me! She abused me! She attempted to cover up her ... her licentious behavior by fabricating her husband was with her."

Karl took a step toward her, his fists clenched at his side as he took in deep gulps of air. "I was with her. And you have no right to speak about my wife in that way. She is a fine, honorable woman. Only a woman lacking in her own honor would wish my Leena any harm."

Mrs. Jameson blanched as she looked around the group now circling Leena with their support. She cast a glance at the townsfolk, watching the spectacle she had created, finding few sympathetic to her cause. She bristled with indignation. "You think you can demand that I pay a penny to that worthless Improvement Committee fund?"

Warren lowered his voice so it was heard only among their immediate group. "Either you pay to the fund or I will ensure you are beggared." His eyes shone with his distaste. "Think carefully, Mrs. Jameson, for I doubt you have many friends who will come forth and speak in your favor."

Mrs. Jameson blanched and backed away. "You will pay for what you've done to me."

Warren shook his head as he saw Leena leaning against Karl as she battled her distress and felt his own wife trembling beside him. "We already have."

Mrs. Jameson glared at the unified group before spinning on her heels and marching away.

"That was singularly unpleasant," Annabelle muttered.

"There isna one of us who that woman hasna attempted to harm or malign with her vicious words," Alistair said as he ran a hand over Leticia's shoulder.

Warren smiled. "I wouldn't worry about her. She's discovering just how few friends she has in town. She'll pay the fine and agree to the terms for she has no desire to be forced from her home of many years."

"Aye, but it willna stop the woman's penchant for mischief," Ewan muttered.

Karl grumbled. "Only when she's dead will that end." He flushed as he saw Helen flinch. "I beg your pardon."

Helen shook her head and gave a weak smile to the group. "No, I'm sorry. I wish …"

Leena gripped her arm. "She is nothing more than an irritation to Karl and me. We are fine. Her words will not hurt us."

Helen breathed a sigh of relief, and her smile broadened at Leena's reassurance.

Jessamine sighed as she tracked Mrs. Jameson's movements, Jessamine's gaze finally darting back to the group after Mrs. Jameson departed the Hall. "I fear she will find a way to cause mischief for Sorcha. The longer she is at the ranch, the louder the rumors of impropriety will grow."

Cailean gave a small groan and shook his head. "Can we not enjoy tonight without worrying about tomorrow?"

"Aye," Alistair said. "Tomorrow's problems will come soon enough."

They were interrupted from saying anything further as Harold quieted the musicians and spoke in a loud voice to attract the towns-folk's attention. He wore his best suit and a red waistcoat. "Thank you for joining us tonight for our Second Annual Bear Grass Springs'

New Year's Eve Dance!" He smiled and gave a small bow as a few of the miners whistled.

"The man should be mayor," Ewan muttered, earning a grunt of agreement from his brothers.

"As you know, we are attempting to fatten the coffers of our sparsely funded Bear Grass Springs' Improvement Committee." He smiled and stepped aside from the gingerbread house. "With that in mind, we are going to auction off this delicious edible treat prepared by our very own Leena Johansen."

The crowd gave an appreciative murmur at the large house with multicolored icing. Leena flushed and nodded as the townsfolk looked in her direction.

"I hear it is like one large gingerbread cookie!" Harold proclaimed with glee.

"*Ja*," Leena said and smiled as interest in her gingerbread house grew at that proclamation.

"Therefore, I'll start the bidding at five dollars. We must be generous as we fund our Improvement Committee!"

"They'll never receive so much money," Leena protested to Karl.

Karl kissed her head and whispered in her ear, "Watch and listen. Cailean told me that Harold is a master at auctions."

Soon the bidding had risen to thirty dollars. Ewan silently nodded as each bid was made, but, after the bid surpassed twenty, Jessamine whispered in his ear, and he dropped out. Finally Harold called out, "Going once. ... Going twice. ... Sold for twenty-five dollars!" He pointed to a miner wearing a fine suit, and the townsfolk clapped.

"He must have had a bit of luck," Annabelle said.

Leena shook her head in surprise. "I never thought anyone would pay such money."

"I'm sorry, love," Ewan said as he kissed Jessamine's forehead.

Jessamine smiled and kissed his cheek. "Thank you for being gallant and attempting to purchase me that gingerbread house." She watched as the miner called his friends over, and they began to nibble at it.

Leena looked at her friends and smiled. "Don't fret," she whispered. "You're friends with a baker."

Cailean nodded. "Aye, with two," he said as he squeezed Annabelle.

"And, with friends like us, you'll never go hungry for treats," Leena teased. Soon she joined Karl on the dance floor as the musicians played a slow waltz. "Thank you," she whispered.

"For what, *min kjærlighet?*" He smiled as she flushed at his saying "my love" in Norwegian.

"For standing beside me. For not allowing Mrs. Jameson's words to separate us." She smiled as his gaze softened. "For not ruining our surprise for our friends when they arrive home tonight."

Karl laughed. "I wish I could see their faces when they realize they have small *pepperkake* houses waiting for them."

"Nathanial was good to agree to deliver them for us."

"*Ja*, and we're lucky the MacKinnons don't lock their doors," he said with a smile.

She leaned her head against his shoulder. "This has been the best Christmas and New Year's, Karl. Thank you."

He grinned at her. "It's our first of many." He leaned forward and kissed her softly on the lips before pulling her tightly against his chest. He held her close as they slowly moved around the dance floor.

Later that evening, after riding home from the dance with Nathanial, Leena entered the small house she shared with her husband, her hands shaking from the cold and her nervousness. She watched as he stoked the fire in the stove, her eyes tracking how his muscles flexed with the movement.

He turned and caught her staring. He smiled and winked at her. When she flushed and wrung her hands, he frowned. "Leena, love, why are you standing by the door, still with your coat on?" He moved to her and helped her out of her outerwear as though she were a child. When he noted her shivering, he tugged her to the warming stove.

"No," she rasped, when he moved away, clinging to him. "Hold me."

She pushed herself into his arms, holding him tight. "I need to feel your arms around me."

"What happened?" he whispered. "Whatever it is, it will be all right. You know that woman will not harm us, *ja*? And we had a wonderful time with our friends." He held her, rocking her to and fro as they stood in front of the stove. He slowly began to twirl them in a circle so they both warmed, and his deep voice hummed a Norwegian lullaby to her. When he realized she was crying, his hold on her tightened. "Please, my love, what is it?"

"I love our home," she said into his ear. "I will miss it when we have to move."

He chuckled. "We won't have to move until we have a ..." He froze, their impromptu dance abruptly halted. He pushed her away, his thumbs chasing tears down her cheeks. "Leena?"

She smiled and nodded. After sharing a long glance, she turned her cheek and kissed his palm. Then she picked it up and placed it over her belly. "*Ja*, a *spebarn*. In summer."

He dropped to his knees, hugging her close as he wrapped his arms around her lower back, his face buried against her belly as he kissed it. "A baby. Oh, I never dared dream I'd be a father."

She giggled as her fingers tangled in his blond hair. "With what we've done since we married, it was bound to occur."

His raised brilliant, hope-filled eyes to meet hers. "Thank you."

She dropped to her knees, kissing him. "We will be wonderful parents, Karl. You will be such a magnificent father." She let out a hitching breath as her tears abated.

His gaze held fear and hope in equal measure. "Do you believe that?"

She cupped his cheeks and met his gaze. "Yes. I trust you. I love you. And I know you will only show love and dedication to our child. To our children."

"Yes," he rasped as he tugged her close. After many moments he whispered, "Why were you crying?" He gave her a gentle squeeze. "Truly?"

"Today, when we were at the dance, I overheard Cailean whisper

115

to Alistair about Jessamine losing a baby." Leena leaned away and kissed Karl's cheek as she met his gaze. "I was standing here in our home, so happy with my surprise for you and yet filled with such sadness for them." She attempted a smile as her tears fell again. "I can't imagine how sad Jessamine is."

Karl shuddered as he pulled Leena close, sitting on the floor with her between his strong legs. "And Ewan. Always so happy. I wondered why he was not more jovial at Christmas. He seemed better today, although he still looked like he mourned something." Karl held Leena, rocking side to side subtly. "Never doubt that I want you more than any baby we might have." He moved so she could see his earnest expression. "I want our baby, *ja*, but not more than I want you."

"Oh, Karl," she whispered. "Thank you for being my husband. For having the courage to confront your past and to realize that you are more than the people who raised you ever knew you could be."

He smiled and traced a finger over her cheek. "Your love, Leena, your faith in me, gave me the strength I needed to be more." He frowned as she shook her head.

"No." She kissed his palm. "No, it gave you the freedom to be who you always were. I love you as you are, not as I wish you were."

He groaned and kissed her passionately. They broke apart, and he whispered, "Together, my love, we will have such a wonderful life. You enjoying your work at the bakery while I work with your brother and our children grow up all around us."

She sniffled and smiled as she snuggled into his embrace. "Always together."

~

Never Fear! There are more Bear Grass Springs books coming! Look for Sorcha and Frederick's Novel- *Montana Wrangler* in January 2019—read on for a sneak peek and preorder now!

Look for Fidelia and Bears' Novel- in March 2019.

SNEAK PEEK: MONTANA WRANGLER

Bear Grass Springs, Montana, November 1886

EXCERPT FROM CHAPTER ONE

*I*t was an inauspicious way to die. Sorcha MacKinnon stared at the blue sky overhead yet watched the storm clouds nearing as the snow-covered branches of the pine trees swayed in the breeze. She took a deep breath and tried to move, biting back a scream of pain as she barely progressed an inch. "Sugar?" she called out to her horse.

She closed her eyes and listened for any sound, tears coursing from her eyes and wetting her hair. "Why should I want a horse that threw me?" she said in a quavering voice. She continued to mutter to herself so she didn't feel so alone in the large, empty forest.

Her eyes snapped open at a creaking sound, her heart racing. A strange snip of a memory came to her. *She died too soon.* Her heart raced and breath emerged as pants as she strained to remember anything further. After a moment, she took a deep breath, realizing the pine tree had made the noise after a strong gust of wind blew snow off its branches. In her pain-induced state, her mind jumped from memories of holding her niece, Skye, to arguing with her youngest brother, Ewan, to laughing with her sisters-in-law at the bakery. "I dinna want to die alone." She tried to move again and fainted from the pain.

~

Frederick Tompkins paused on his way from the ranch house to the horse barn to watch the large fluffy white clouds move across the brilliant blue Montana sky, followed by a band of darker storm clouds. Along with his two brothers, Peter and Cole, Frederick ran the Mountain Bluebird Ranch, or MBR.

Near the main ranch house stood two large barns. One housed Frederick's prize horses, while the other held milk cows, goats and pigs. In front of the horse barn was the blacksmith shop with a hand pump for water. Large interconnecting paddocks and corrals were behind the barns and to the side of the larger horse barn.

Frederick pulled on his hat and strode to the barn. The MBR was the largest and most successful cattle ranch in the valley near Bear Grass Springs, Montana. His grandparents and father had founded it in the 1860s and then given it to the three brothers. Whereas Frederick chose to remain in Montana, Cole and Peter preferred the adventure of driving herds up from Texas each spring. They were currently in Chicago with the cattle they had cut from the herd to sell. Frederick knew from previous years' experience that his brothers would return to Texas rather than winter in Montana.

He smiled to himself as he considered winter in Montana. Rather than look to a calendar to determine the season, Montanans often joked there were two seasons, summer and winter, with winter lasting up to six months. He glanced at the foreboding dark clouds on the horizon again, and he knew that winter was about to arrive. He said a silent prayer that it would be a mild one like last year's.

Frederick gave a small grunt of satisfaction that his brothers had missed the recent harvest dance held in town. Frederick glowered as he thought about the dance he had shared with Sorcha MacKinnon.

He tugged at his red bandanna tied around his neck, flushing as he remembered storming away from her after she had called him a "simple-minded wrangler." Her mocking stare as she intimated any woman living on his ranch would be miserable had filled him with such ire that he had been unable to speak.

A cool breeze blew, scattering fallen leaves and rustling the prairie grass poking through the light skiff of snow, helping to cool his momentary anger at the memory. After the long harsh summer, the grass was thin and sparse on the range, with little for the cattle to eat over the coming winter months. Fresh snow shone like a beacon on the nearby mountain peaks with the hint of more snow to come in the air itself as well as in the nearing clouds. He focused on the land around him, forcefully putting his memory of Sorcha from his mind.

Frederick called out to Dalton, one of his hands. "I'm taking Boots out for a ride. To clear my head and let her run before the storm hits. Might be my last chance to roam the range before winter arrives." He rubbed a hand along the neck of one of his prized horses, a beautiful chestnut filly with white forelocks. He clicked and murmured, "Come on, Boots. Let's see how fast you want to run." Although a cattle ranch, Frederick raised prized horses and had begun to earn a reputation for them in the area.

He barreled down the drive before slowing Boots to a trot and veering off onto his land as they headed toward the mountains. Boots tossed her head as though upset with the slowing of their pace before she settled into a gentle canter. The frost on the grass melted as the day warmed, and Frederick saw hawks circling overhead in search of any small creature foolish enough to be on the prairie. Few of his cattle were visible as they had scattered on the range after the fall roundup last month. He stared in dismay at the brittle grass and prayed for a mild winter.

As he followed a well-worn trail, Frederick's sense of unease heightened rather than diminished. The trees thickened as he approached the base of the mountains, and he heard the soft trickle of a nearby stream. The air cooled, and the scent on the breeze was sweeter with the fresh smell of pine trees mixed with mossy undertones from the creek. He paused Boots, closing his eyes to breathe deeply as worries about the ranch and his fledgling horse business faded. The soft wind moved through the trees and caressed his hair and face, further easing his tension. After a few more moments, he patted Boots's neck and was about to turn for home when he saw a piece of green fabric on a rock.

He jumped from his horse to pick it up and then heard a sound. He closed his eyes. A moan. After a moment, he heard a whimper. Walking with Boots's bridle in his hand, Frederick turned the corner of the trail and came to an abrupt halt. Someone lay crumpled in front of him, and he took a deep breath after seeing the figure move.

"Don't be frightened," Frederick whispered.

"Dinna touch me!" Her voice emerged, tremulous, weak and pain-ladened.

"Sorcha?" He tied his horse to a nearby tree and dropped to his haunches. He ran a hand over her head and back, frowning when his hand came away blood-stained. "Let me turn you over."

"Dinna touch me," she said again as a sob burst forth. "It hurts too much. Just let me die."

"You dramatic fool," he muttered. "I won't let you die in the wilderness, a target for the wolves and bears. Is that how you'd like to meet your maker?" He waited until he saw a small shrug of her shoulders. "Is that your greatest desire? To become a tall tale in Jessamine's newspaper?" Sorcha MacKinnon, the only unmarried MacKinnon in Bear Grass Springs, had arrived from the Isle of Skye in Scotland two years ago to join her brothers Cailean, Alistair and Ewan. The youngest brother, Ewan, was married to Jessamine, the town's reporter.

Sorcha pushed herself up enough to glare at Frederick, her light blue eyes lit with animosity. "How dare ye turn what has happened to me into a farce?"

"I'm not the one begging to be left in the wilderness to die." He reached forward and eased her onto her back, earning a yelp of surprise before she passed out. "Sorcha!" he screamed. "Sorcha!"

She was as white as a freshly bleached sheet, and he frantically placed his fingers at her throat, anxious to feel any sign of life. He leaned over her, his breath calming as he felt her soft exhalations on his cheek. "Wake up, you devilish woman." He ran a hand over her arms and then blanched as her burgundy wool skirt had risen up one leg, and he saw the odd angle of her upper right leg. "Oh, dear God, what have you done?"

"I dinna do anything," she whispered, her eyes still closed. "It was Sugar. She bolted and threw me. Somehow I hit a rock, and ... I dinna remember the rest."

"You could have broken your neck."

"Aye." She took a deep breath, her mouth tight with pain. "Then I wouldna be in such pain."

Frederick made a noise of disgust that rivaled any noise her Scottish brothers made. "Do you think your family wouldn't mourn you? How could you be so selfish?"

Tears seeped out of the corner of her eyes. "I ken I have a broken leg, Frederick. I ken I'll be a cripple the rest of my life." She swallowed a sob. "I dinna want that." Until this moment, they had always snarled and circled around each other when they met at his grandparents' café or at a town dance.

He leaned forward and swiped at her cheeks, meeting her startled gaze at his tender touch. "You will not die. You will not be crippled. You are strong and determined and as irascible as anyone I've ever met." He looked deeply into her eyes. "You will fight."

She nodded and then flushed. "Dinna tell them I was so weak, aye?"

He smiled. "Never." He looked to his horse and then at Sorcha. "I can't get you to the ranch with a broken leg on my horse." He pulled off his long jacket and covered her and then tugged the bandanna from around his neck, tying it to help staunch the bleeding at the back of her head. "I have to leave you to get help."

Her eyes were frantic before she closed them and nodded. "Aye, I understand." She opened them as she felt him place a revolver in one of her hands.

"I hope you have a basic understanding of how to use this." At her nod, he squeezed her arm. "I'll return as soon as I can, and I'll call out, so you will know it's me."

"Hurry," she whispered.

He leaned forward and kissed her on her forehead. "Fight, Sorcha." He rose, grabbed his horse's reins and was off before she could react to his impetuous action.

Preorder Now- Available January 2019!

ALSO BY RAMONA FLIGHTNER

BEAR GRASS SPRINGS SERIES

Montana Untamed

Montana Grit

Montana Maverick

Montana Renegade

Montana Wrangler- coming in January 2019!

THE BANISHED SAGA

Banished Love

Reclaimed Love

Undaunted Love, Part One

Undaunted Love, Part Two

Tenacious Love

With Many More!

AFTERWORD

Hi!

Thank you for reading Leena and Karl's story! I hope you enjoyed reading it as much as I enjoyed writing it. I loved researching Norwegian Christmas customs and finding their way to happily ever after. You'll read much more about the harsh winter of 1886/87 in Sorcha and Frederick's upcoming novel!

During my research, I found that *spebarn* meant baby or infant while *spedbarn* meant infants or babies. I hope this is correct and know that any Norwegian errors are mine.

As for the Bear Grass Springs Series, there are many more books to come! Sorcha and Frederick's novel will be available in January 2019, Bears and Fidelia's will be available in March 2019 with many more after that! Thank you for joining me in this adventure.

If you want to stay up to date with new releases, cover reveals and special treats I only send to my newsletter subscribers, sign up now!

AFTERWORD

Happy Reading,

Ramona

ABOUT THE AUTHOR

Ramona is a historical romance author who loves to immerse herself in research as much as she loves writing. A native of Montana, every day she marvels that she gets to live in such a beautiful place. When she's not writing, her favorite pastimes are fly fishing the cool clear streams of a Montana river, hiking in the mountains, and spending time with family and friends.

Ramona's heroines are strong, resilient women, the type of women you'd love to have as your best friend. Her heroes are loyal and honorable, of men you'd love to meet or bring home to introduce to your family for Sunday dinner. She hopes her stories bring the past alive and allow you to forget the outside world for a while.

BB bookbub.com/authors/ramona-flightner

f facebook.com/authorramonaflightner

instagram.com/rflightner

pinterest.com/Ramonaauthor